The Empty Hours

Ed McBain was born in Manhattan, but fled to the Bronx at the age of twelve. He went through elementary and high school in the New York school system, and the Navy claimed him in 1944. When he returned two years later, he attended Hunter College. After a variety of jobs, he worked for a literary agent, where he learnt about plotting stories. When his agent-boss started selling them regularly to magazines, and sold a mystery novel and a juvenile science-fiction title as well, they both decided that it would be more profitable for him to stay at home and write full time.

Under his own name, Evan Hunter, he is the author of a number of novels, including *The Blackboard Jungle*, *Come Winter* and *Every Little Crook and Nanny*. As Ed McBain he has written the highly popular '87th Precinct' series of crime novels, including *Shotgun, Jigsaw, Fuzz, Hail, Hail, The Gang's All Here, Sadie When She Died*, and *Calypso*, all of which are available in Pan.

Ed McBain

The Empty Hours

87th Precinct Mysteries

Pan Books London and Sydney

First published in Great Britain 1981 by Pan Books Ltd,
Cavaye Place, London SW10 9PG
© Ed McBain 1960, 1961, 1962
ISBN 0 330 26279 3
Set in Linotype Times by
Northumberland Press Ltd, Gateshead, Tyne and Wear
Made and printed in Great Britain by
Richard Clay (The Chaucer Press) Ltd,
Bungay, Suffolk

This is for Howard Melnick –
my brother-in-law

The city in these pages is imaginary.
The people, the places are all fictitious.
Only the police routine is based on
established investigatory technique.

The Empty Hours

1

They thought she was coloured at first.

The patrolman who investigated the complaint didn't expect to find a dead woman. This was the first time he'd seen a corpse, and he was somewhat shaken by the ludicrously relaxed grotesqueness of the girl lying on her back on the rug, and his hand trembled a little as he made out his report. But when he came to the blank line calling for an identification of RACE, he unhesitatingly wrote 'Negro'.

The call had been taken at Headquarters by a patrolman in the central Complaint Bureau. He sat at a desk with a pad of printed forms before him, and he copied down the information, shrugged because this seemed like a routine squeal, rolled the form and slipped it into a metal carrier, and then shot it by pneumatic tube to the radio room. A dispatcher there read the complaint form, shrugged because this seemed like a routine squeal, studied the precinct map on the wall opposite his desk, and then dispatched car eleven of the 87th Precinct to the scene.

The girl was dead.

She may have been a pretty girl, but she was hideous in death, distorted by the expanding gases inside her skin case. She was wearing a sweater and skirt, and she was barefoot, and her skirt had been pulled back when she fell to the rug. Her head was twisted at a curious angle, the short black hair cradled by the rug, her eyes open and brown in a bloated

9

face. The patrolman felt a sudden impulse to pull the girl's skirt down over her knees. He knew, suddenly, she would have wanted this. Death had caught her in this indecent posture, robbing her of female instinct. There were things this girl would never do again, so many things, all of which must have seemed enormously important to the girl herself. But the single universal thing was an infinitesimal detail, magnified now by death: she would never again perform the simple feminine and somehow beautiful act of pulling her skirt down over her knees.

The patrolman sighed and finished his report. The image of the dead girl remained in his mind all the way down to the squad car.

It was hot in the squadroom on that night in early August. The men working the graveyard shift had reported for duty at 6.00 p.m., and they would not go home until eight the following morning. They were all detectives and perhaps privileged members of the police force, but there were many policemen – Detective Meyer Meyer among them – who maintained that a uniformed cop's life made a hell of a lot more sense than a detective's.

'Sure, it does,' Meyer insisted now, sitting at his desk in his shirt sleeves. 'A patrolman's schedule provides regularity and security. It gives a man a home life.'

'This squadroom is your home, Meyer,' Carella said. 'Admit it.'

'Sure,' Meyer answered, grinning. 'I can't wait to come to work each day.' He passed a hand over his bald pate. 'You know what I like especially about this place? The interior decoration. The décor. It's very restful.'

'Oh, you don't like your fellow workers, huh?' Carella said. He slid off the desk and winked at Cotton Hawes, who was standing at one of the filing cabinets. Then he walked towards the water cooler at the other end of the room, just inside the slatted railing that divided squadroom from corridor. He moved with a nonchalant ease that was deceptive. Steve Carella had never been one of those weightlifting goons, and the image he presented was hardly one of bulging muscular power. But there was a quiet strength about the man and the way he moved, a confidence in the way he casually accepted the capabilities and limitations of his body. He stopped at the water cooler, filled a paper cup, and turned to look at Meyer again.

'No, I like my colleagues,' Meyer said. 'In fact, Steve, if I had my choice in all the world of who to work with, I would choose you honourable, decent guys. Sure.' Meyer nodded, building steam. 'In fact, I'm thinking of having some medals cast off, so I can hand them out to you guys. Boy, am I lucky to have this job! I may come to work without pay from now on. I may just refuse my salary, this job is so enriching. I want to thank you guys. You make me recognize the real values in life.'

'He makes a nice speech,' Hawes said.

'He should run the line-up. It would break the monotony. How come you don't run the line-up, Meyer?'

'Steve, I been offered the job,' Meyer said seriously. 'I told them I'm needed right here at the Eighty-seventh, the garden spot of all the precincts. Why, they offered me chief of detectives, and when I said no, they offered me commissioner, but I was loyal to the squad.'

'Let's give *him* a medal,' Hawes said, and the telephone rang.

Meyer lifted the receiver. 'Eighty-seventh Squad, Detective Meyer. What? Yeah, just a second.' He pulled a pad into place and began writing. 'Yeah, I got it. Right. Right. Right. Okay.' He hung up. Carella had walked to his desk. 'A little coloured girl,' Meyer said.

'Yeah?'

'In a furnished room on South Eleventh.'

'Yeah?'

'Dead,' Meyer said.

2

The city doesn't seem to be itself in the very early hours of the morning.

She is a woman, of course, and time will never change that. She awakes as a woman, tentatively touching the day in a yawning, smiling stretch, her lips free of colour, her hair tousled, warm from sleep, her body richer, an innocent girlish quality about her as sunlight stains the eastern sky and covers her with early heat. She dresses in furnished rooms in crummy rundown slums, and she dresses in Hall Avenue penthouses, and in the countless apartments that crowd the buildings of Isola and Riverhead and Calm's Point, in the private houses that line the streets of Bethtown and Majesta, and she emerges a different woman, sleek and businesslike, attractive but not sexy, a look of utter competence about her, manicured and polished, but with no time for nonsense, there is a long working day ahead of her. At five o'clock a metamorphosis takes place. She does not change her costume, this city, this woman, she wears the same frock or the same suit, the same high-heeled pumps or the same suburban loafers, but something breaks through that immaculate shell, a mood, a tone, an undercurrent. She is a different woman who sits in the bars and cocktail lounges, who relaxes on the patios or on the terraces shelving the skyscrapers, a different woman with a somewhat lazily inviting grin, a somewhat tired expression, an impenetrable knowledge on her face and in her eyes: she lifts her glass, she laughs gently, the evening sits expectantly on the skyline, the sky is awash with the purple of day's end.

She turns female in the night.

She drops her femininity and turns female. The polish is gone, the mechanized competence; she becomes a little scatterbrained and a little cuddly; she crosses her legs recklessly and allows her lipstick to be kissed clear off her mouth, and she responds to the male hands on her body, and she turns soft and inviting and miraculously primitive. The night is a female time, and the city is nothing but a woman.

And in the empty hours she sleeps, and she does not seem to be herself.

In the morning she will awake again and touch the silent air in a yawn, spreading her arms, the contented smile on her naked mouth. Her hair will be mussed, we will know her, we have seen her this way often.

But now she sleeps. She sleeps silently, this city. Oh, an eye open in the buildings of the night here and there, winking on, off again, silence. She rests. In sleep we do not recognize her. Her sleep is not like death, for we can hear and sense the murmur of life beneath the warm bedclothes. But she is a strange woman whom we have known intimately, loved passionately, and now she curls into an unresponsive ball beneath the sheets, and our hand is on her rich hip. We can feel life there, but we do not know her. She is faceless and featureless in the dark. She could be any city, any woman, anywhere. We touch her uncertainly. She has pulled the black nightgown of early morning around her, and we do not know her. She is a stranger, and her eyes are closed.

The landlady was frightened by the presence of policemen, even though she had summoned them. The taller one, the one who called himself Detective Hawes, was a redheaded giant with a white streak in his hair, a horror if she'd ever seen one. The landlady stood in the apartment where the girl lay dead on the rug, and she talked to the detectives in whispers, not because she was in the presence of death, but only because it was three o'clock in the morning. The landlady was wearing a bathrobe over her gown. There was an intimacy to the scene, the same intimacy that hangs alike over an impending fishing trip or a completed tragedy. Three a.m. is a time for slumber, and those who are awake while the city sleeps share a common bond that makes them friendly aliens.

'What's the girl's name?' Carella asked. It was three o'clock in the morning, and he had not shaved since five p.m. the day before, but his chin looked smooth. His eyes slanted slightly downward, combining with his clean-shaven face to give him a curiously oriental appearance. The landlady liked him. He was a nice boy, she thought. In her lexicon the men of the world were either 'nice boys' or 'louses'. She wasn't sure about Cotton Hawes yet, but she imagined he was a parasitic insect.

'Claudia Davis,' she answered, directing the answer to Carella whom she liked, and totally ignoring Hawes who had no right to be so big a man with a frightening white streak in his hair.

'Do you know how old she was?' Carella asked.

'Twenty-eight or twenty-nine, I think.'

'Had she been living here long?'

'Since June,' the landlady said.

'That short a time, huh?'

'And *this* has to happen,' the landlady said. 'She seemed like such a nice girl. Who do you suppose did it?'

'I don't know,' Carella said.

'Or do you think it was suicide? I don't smell no gas, do you?'

'No,' Carella said. 'Do you know where she lived before this, Mrs Mauder?'

'No, I don't.'

'You didn't ask for references when she took the apartment?'

'It's only a furnished room,' Mrs Mauder said, shrugging. 'She paid me a month's rent in advance.'

'How much was that, Mrs Mauder?'

'Sixty dollars. She paid it in cash. I never take cheques from strangers.'

'But you have no idea whether she's from this city, or out of town, or whatever. Am I right?'

'Yes, that's right.'

'Davis,' Hawes said, shaking his head. 'That'll be a tough name to track down, Steve. Must be a thousand of them in the phone book.'

'Why is your hair white?' the landlady asked.

'Huh?'

'That streak.'

'Oh.' Hawes unconsciously touched his left temple. 'I got

knifed once,' he said, dismissing the question abruptly. 'Mrs Mauder, was the girl living alone?'

'I don't know. I mind my own business.'

'Well, surely you would have seen ...'

'I think she was living alone. I don't pry, and I don't spy. She gave me a month's rent in advance.'

Hawes sighed. He could feel the woman's hostility. He decided to leave the questioning to Carella. 'I'll take a look through the drawers and closets,' he said, and moved off without waiting for Carella's answer.

'It's awfully hot in here,' Carella said.

'The patrolman said we shouldn't touch anything until you got here,' Mrs Mauder said. 'That's why I didn't open the windows or nothing.'

'That was very thoughtful of you,' Carella said, smiling. 'But I think we can open the window now, don't you?'

'If you like. It does smell in here. Is ... is that her? Smelling?'

'Yes,' Carella answered. He pulled open the window. 'There. That's a little better.'

'Doesn't help much,' the landlady said. 'The weather's been terrible – just terrible. Body can't sleep at all.' She looked down at the dead girl. 'She looks just awful, don't she?'

'Yes. Mrs Mauder, would you know where she worked, or if she had a job?'

'No, I'm sorry.'

'Anyone ever come by asking for her? Friends? Relatives?'

'No, I'm sorry. I never saw any.'

'Can you tell me anything about her habits? When she left the house in the morning? When she returned at night?'

'I'm sorry; I never noticed.'

'Well, what made you think something was wrong in here?'

'The milk. Outside the door. I was out with some friends tonight, you see, and when I came back a man on the third floor called down to say his neighbour was playing the radio very loud and would I tell him to shut up, please. So I went upstairs and asked him to turn down the radio, and then I passed Miss Davis' apartment and saw the milk standing outside the door, and I thought this was kind of funny in such hot weather, but I figured it was *her* milk, you know, and I don't like to pry. So I came down and went to bed, but I couldn't stop thinking about that milk standing outside in the hallway. So I put on a robe and came upstairs and knocked on the door, and she didn't answer. So I called out to her, and she still didn't answer. So I figured something must be wrong. I don't know why. I just figured ... I don't know. If she was in here, why didn't she answer?'

'How'd you know she was here?'

'I didn't.'

'Was the door locked?'

'Yes.'

'You tried it?'

'Yes. It was locked.'

'I see,' Carella said.

'Couple of cars just pulled up downstairs,' Hawes said, walking over. 'Probably the lab. And Homicide South.'

'They know the squeal is ours,' Carella said. 'Why do they bother?'

'Make it look good,' Hawes said. 'Homicide's got the title on the door, so they figure they ought to go out and earn their salaries.'

'Did you find anything?'

'A brand-new set of luggage in the closet, six pieces. The drawers and closets are full of clothes. Most of them look new. Lots of resort stuff, Steve. Found some brand-new books, too.'

'What else?'

'Some mail on the dresser top.'

'Anything we can use?'

Hawes shrugged. 'A statement from the girl's bank. Bunch of cancelled cheques. Might help us.'

'Maybe,' Carella said. 'Let's see what the lab comes up with.'

The laboratory report came the next day, together with a necropsy report from the assistant medical examiner. In combination, the reports were fairly valuable. The first thing the detectives learned was that the girl was a white Caucasian of approximately thirty years of age.

Yes, white.

The news came as something of a surprise to the cops because the girl lying on the rug had certainly looked like a Negress. After all, her skin was black. Not tan, not coffee-coloured, not brown, but black – that intensely black coloration found in primitive tribes who spend a good deal of their time in the sun. The conclusion seemed to be a logical one, but death is a great equalizer not without a whimsical humour all its own, and the funniest kind of joke is a sight gag. Death changes white to black, and when that grisly old man comes marching in there's no question of who's going to school with whom. There's no longer any question of pigmentation, friend. The girl on the floor looked black, but she was white, and whatever else she was she was also stone cold dead, and that's the worst you can do to anybody.

The report explained that the girl's body was in a state of advanced putrefaction, and it went into such esoteric terms as 'general distention of the body cavities, tissues, and blood vessels with gas', and 'black discoloration of the skin, mucous membranes, and irides caused by haemolysis and action of hydrogen sulphide on the blood pigment', all of which broke down to the simple fact that it was a damn hot week in August and the girl had been lying on a rug which retained heat and speeded the post-mortem putrefaction. From what they could tell, and in weather like this, it was mostly a guess, the girl had been dead and decomposing for at least forty-eight hours, which set the time of her demise as August first or thereabouts.

One of the reports went on to say that the clothes she'd been wearing had been purchased in one of the city's larger department stores. All of her clothes – those she wore and those found in her apartment – were rather expensive, but someone at the lab thought it necessary to note that all her panties were trimmed with Belgian lace and retailed for twenty-five dollars a pair. Someone else at the lab mentioned that a thorough examination of her garments and her body had revealed no traces of blood, semen, or oil stains.

The coroner fixed the cause of death as strangulation.

3

It is amazing how much an apartment can sometimes yield to science. It is equally amazing, and more than a little disappointing, to get nothing from the scene of a murder when you are desperately seeking a clue. The furnished room in which Claudia Davis had been strangled to death was full of juicy surfaces conceivably carrying hundreds of latent fingerprints. The closets and drawers contained piles of clothing that might have carried traces of anything from gunpowder to face powder.

But the lab boys went around lifting their prints and sifting their dust and vacuuming with a Söderman-Heuberger filter, and they went down to the morgue and studied the girl's skin and came up with a total of nothing. Zero. Oh, not quite zero. They got a lot of prints belonging to Claudia Davis, and a lot of dust collected from all over the city and clinging to her shoes and her furniture. They also found some documents belonging to the dead girl – a birth certificate, a diploma of graduation from a high school in Santa Monica, and an expired library card. And, oh, yes, a key. The key didn't seem to fit any of the locks in the room. They sent all the junk over to the 87th, and Sam Grossman called Carella personally later that day to apologize for the lack of results.

The squadroom was hot and noisy when Carella took the call from the lab. The conversation was a curiously one-sided affair. Carella, who had dumped the contents of the laboratory envelope on to his desk, merely grunted or nodded every now and then. He thanked Grossman at last, hung up, and stared at the window facing the street and Grover Park.

'Get anything?' Meyer asked.

'Yeah. Grossman thinks the killer was wearing gloves.'

'That's nice,' Meyer said.

'Also, I think I know what this key is for.' He lifted it from the desk.

'Yeah? What?'

'Well, did you see these cancelled cheques?'

'No.'

'Take a look,' Carella said.

He opened the brown bank envelope addressed to Claudia Davis, spread the cancelled cheques on his desk top, and then unfolded the yellow bank statement. Meyer studied the display silently.

'Cotton found the envelope in her room,' Carella said. 'The statement covers the month of July. Those are all the cheques she wrote, or at least everything that cleared the bank by the thirty-first.'

'Lots of cheques here,' Meyer said.

'Twenty-five, to be exact. What do you think? I know what *I* think,' Carella said.

'What's that?'

'I look at those cheques, I can see a life. It's like reading someone's diary. Everything she did last month is right here, Meyer. All the department stores she went to, look, a florist, her hairdresser, a candy shop, even her shoemaker, and look at this. A cheque made out to a funeral home. Now who died, Meyer, huh? And look here. She was living at Mrs Mauder's place, but here's a cheque made out to a swank apartment building on the South Side, in Stewart City. And some of these cheques are just made out to names, *people*. This case is crying for some people.'

'You want me to get the phone book?'

'No, wait a minute. Look at this bank statement. She opened the account on July fifth with a thousand bucks. All of a sudden, bam, she deposits a thousand bucks in the seaboard Bank of America.'

'What's so odd about that?'

'Nothing, maybe. But Cotton called the other banks in the city, and Claudia Davis has a very healthy account at the Highland Trust on Cromwell Avenue. And I mean *very* healthy.'

'How healthy?'

'Close to sixty grand.'

'What!'

'You heard me. And the Highland Trust lists no withdrawals for the month of July. So where'd she get the money to put into Seaboard?'

'Was that the only deposit?'

'Take a look.'

Meyer picked up the statement.

'The initial deposit was on July fifth,' Carella said. 'A thousand bucks. She made another thousand-dollar deposit on July twelfth. And another on the nineteenth. And another on the twenty-seventh.'

Meyer raised his eyebrows. 'Four grand. That's a lot of loot.'

'And all deposited in less than a month's time. I've got to work almost a full year to make that kind of money.'

'Not to mention the sixty grand in the other bank. Where do you suppose she got it, Steve?'

'I don't know. It just doesn't make sense. She wears underpants trimmed with Belgian lace, but she lives in a crummy room-and-a-half with bath. How the hell do you figure that? Two bank accounts, twenty-five bucks to cover her ass, and all she pays is sixty bucks a month for a flophouse.'

'Maybe she's hot, Steve.'

'No.' Carella shook his head. 'I ran a make with CBI. She hasn't got a record, and she's not wanted for anything. I haven't heard from the feds yet, but I imagine it'll be the same story.'

'What about that key? You said . . .'

'Oh, yeah. That's pretty simple, thank God. Look at this.'

He reached into the pile of cheques and sorted out a yellow slip, larger than the cheques. He handed it to Meyer. The slip read:

THE SEABOARD BANK OF AMERICA
ISOLA BRANCH
P 1698

July 5

WE ARE CHARGING YOUR ACCOUNT AS PER ITEMS BELOW. PLEASE SEE THAT THE
AMOUNT IS DEDUCTED ON YOUR BOOKS SO THAT OUR ACCOUNTS MAY AGREE.

FOR	Safe deposit rental #375		5	00
	U.S. Tax			50
	AMOUNT OF CHARGE		5	50

CHARGE	Claudia Davis	ENTERED BY
	1263 South Eleventh	
	Isola	*RPL*

'She rented a safe-deposit box the same day she opened the new chequing account, huh?' Meyer said.

'Right.'

'What's in it?'

'That's a good question.'

'Look, do you want to save some time, Steve?'

'Sure.'

'Let's get the court order *before* we go to the bank.'

4

The manager of the Seaboard Bank of America was a bald-headed man in his early fifties. Working on the theory that similar physical types are *simpático*, Carella allowed Meyer to do most of the questioning. It was not easy to elicit answers from Mr Anderson, the manager of the bank, because he was by nature a reticent man. But Detective Meyer Meyer was the most patient man in the city, if not the entire world. His patience was an acquired trait, rather than an inherited one. Oh, he had inherited a few things from his father, a jovial man named Max Meyer, but patience was not one of them. If anything, Max Meyer had been a very impatient if not downright short-tempered sort of fellow. When his wife, for example, came to him with the news that she was expecting a baby, Max nearly hit the ceiling. He enjoyed little jokes immensely, was perhaps the biggest practical joker in all Riverhead, but this particular prank of nature failed to amuse him. He had thought his wife was long past the age when bearing children was even a remote possibility. He never thought of himself as approaching dotage, but he was after all getting on in years, and a change-of-life baby was hardly what the doctor had ordered. He allowed the impending birth to simmer inside him, planning his revenge all the while, plotting the practical joke to end all practical jokes.

When the baby was born, he called it Meyer, a delightful handle which when coupled with the family name provided the infant with a double-barrelled monicker: Meyer Meyer.

Now that's pretty funny. Admit it. You can split your sides laughing over that one, unless you happen to be a pretty sensitive kid who also happens to be an Orthodox Jew, and who happens to live in a predominantly Gentile neighbourhood. The kids in the neighbourhood thought Meyer Meyer had been invented solely for their own pleasure. If they needed further provocation for beating up the Jew boy, and they didn't need any, his name provided excellent motivational fuel. 'Meyer Meyer, Jew on fire!' they would shout, and then they would chase him down the street and beat hell out of him.

Meyer learned patience. It is not very often that one kid, or even one grown man, can successfully defend himself against a gang. But sometimes you can talk yourself out of a beating. Sometimes, if you're patient, if you just wait long enough, you can catch one of them alone and stand up to him face to face, man to man, and know the exultation of a fair fight without the frustration of overwhelming odds.

Listen, Max Meyer's joke was a harmless one. You can't deny an old man his pleasure. But Mr Anderson, the manager of the bank, was fifty-four years old and totally bald. Meyer Meyer, the detective second grade who sat opposite him and asked questions, was also totally bald. Maybe a lifetime of sublimation, a lifetime of devoted patience, doesn't leave any scars. Maybe not. But Meyer Meyer was only thirty-seven years old.

Patiently he said, 'Didn't you find these large deposits rather odd, Mr Anderson?'

'No,' Anderson said. 'A thousand dollars is not a lot of money.'

'Mr Anderson,' Meyer said patiently, 'you are aware, of course, that banks in this city are required to report to the police any unusually large sums of money deposited at one time. You are aware of that, are you not?'

'Yes, I am.'

'Miss Davis deposited four thousand dollars in three weeks' time. Didn't that seem unusual to you?'

'No. The deposits were spaced. A thousand dollars is not a lot of money, and not an unusually large deposit.'

'To me,' Meyer said, 'a thousand dollars is a lot of money. You can buy a lot of beer with a thousand dollars.'

'I don't drink beer,' Anderson said flatly.

'Neither do I,' Meyer answered.

'Besides, we *do* call the police whenever we get a very large deposit, unless the depositor is one of our regular customers. I did not feel that these deposits warranted such a call.'

'Thank you, Mr Anderson,' Meyer said. 'We have a court order here. We'd like to open the box Miss Davis rented.'

'May I see the order, please?' Anderson said. Meyer showed it to him. Anderson sighed and said, 'Very well. Do you have Miss Davis' key?'

Carella reached into his pocket. 'Would this be it?' he said. He put a key on the desk. It was the key that had come to him from the lab together with the documents they'd found in the apartment.

'Yes, that's it,' Mr Anderson said. 'There are two different keys to every box, you see. The bank keeps one, and the renter keeps the other. The box cannot be opened without both keys. Will you come with me, please?'

He collected the bank key to safe-deposit box number 375 and led the detectives to the rear of the bank. The room seemed to be lined with shining metal. The boxes, row upon row, reminded Carella of the morgue and the refrigerated shelves that slid in and out of the wall on squeaking rollers. Anderson pushed the bank key into a slot and turned it, and then he put Claudia Davis' key into a second slot and turned that. He pulled the long, thin box out of the wall and handed it to Meyer. Meyer carried it to the counter on the opposite wall and lifted the catch.

'Okay?' he said to Carella.

'Go ahead.'

Meyer raised the lid of the box.

There was $16,000 in the box. There was also a slip of note paper. The $16,000 was neatly divided into four stacks of bills. Three of the stacks held $5,000 each. The fourth stack held only $1,000. Carella picked up the slip of paper. Someone, presumably Claudia Davis, had made some annotations on it in pencil.

7/5	20,000
7/5	−1,000
	19,000
7/12	−1,000
	18,000
7/19	−1,000
	17,000
7/27	−1,000
	16,000

'Make any sense to you, Mr Anderson?'

'No. I'm afraid not.'

'She came into this bank on July fifth with twenty thousand dollars in cash, Mr Anderson. She put a thousand of that into a chequing account and the remainder into this box. The dates on this slip of paper show exactly when she took cash from the box and transferred it to the chequing account. She knew the rules, Mr Anderson. She knew that twenty grand deposited in one lump would bring a call to the police. This way was a lot safer.'

'We'd better get a list of these serial numbers,' Meyer said.

'Would you have one of your people do that for us, Mr Anderson?'

Anderson seemed ready to protest. Instead, he looked at Carella, sighed, and said, 'Of course.'

The serial numbers didn't help them at all. They compared them against their own lists, and the out-of-town lists, and the FBI lists, but none of those bills was hot.

Only August was.

5

Stewart City hangs in the hair of Isola like a jewelled tiara. Not really a city, not even a town, merely a collection of swank apartment buildings overlooking the River Dix, the community had been named after the British royalty and remained one of the most exclusive neighbourhoods in town. If you could boast of a Stewart City address, you could also boast of a high income, a country place on Sands Spit, and a Mercedes Benz in the garage under the apartment building.

You could give your address with a measure of snobbery and pride – you were, after all, one of the élite.

The dead girl named Claudia Davis had made out a cheque to Management Enterprise, Inc, at 13 Stewart Place South, to the tune of $750. The cheque had been dated July nine, four days after she'd opened the Seaboard account.

A cool breeze was blowing in off the river as Carella and Hawes pulled up. Late-afternoon sunlight dappled the polluted water of the Dix. The bridges connecting Calm's Point with Isola hung against the sky awaiting the assault of dusk.

'Want to pull down the sun visor?' Carella said.

Hawes reached up and turned down the visor. Clipped to the visor so that it showed through the windshield of the car was a hand-lettered card that read POLICEMAN ON DUTY CALL – 87TH PRECINCT. The car, a 1956 Chevrolet, was Carella's own.

'I've got to make a sign for my car,' Hawes said. 'Some bastard tagged it last week.'

'What did you do?'

'I went to court and pleaded not guilty. On my day off.'

'Did you get out of it?'

'Sure. I was answering a squeal. It's bad enough I had to use my own car, but for Pete's sake, to get a ticket!'

'I prefer my own car,' Carella said. 'Those three cars belonging to the squad are ready for the junk heap.'

'*Two*,' Hawes corrected. 'One of them's been in the police garage for a month now.'

'Meyer went down to see about it the other day.'

'What'd they say? Was it ready?'

'No, the mechanic told him there were four patrol cars ahead of the sedan, and they took precedence. Now how about that?'

'Sure, it figures. I've still got a chit in for the gas I used, you know that?'

'Forget it. I've never got back a cent I laid out for gas.'

'What'd Meyer do about the car?'

'He slipped the mechanic five bucks. Maybe that'll speed him up.'

'You know what the city ought to do?' Hawes said. 'They ought to buy some of those used taxicabs. Pick them up for two or three hundred bucks, paint them over, and give them out to the squads. Some of them are still in pretty good condition.'

'Well, it's an idea,' Carella said dubiously, and they entered the building. They found Mrs Miller, the manager, in an office at the rear of the ornate entrance lobby. She was a woman in her early forties with a well-preserved figure and a very husky voice. She wore her hair piled on the top of her head, a pencil stuck rakishly into the reddish-brown heap. She looked at the photostated cheque and said, 'Oh, yes, of course.'

'You knew Miss Davis?'

'Yes, she lived here for a long time.'

'How long?'

'Five years.'

'When did she move out?'

'At the end of June.' Mrs Miller crossed her splendid legs and smiled graciously. The legs were remarkable for a woman of her age, and the smile was almost radiant. She moved with an expert femininity, a calculated, conscious fluidity of flesh that suggested availability and yet was totally respectable. She seemed to have devoted a lifetime to learning the ways and wiles of the female and now practised them with facility and charm. She was pleasant to be with, this woman, pleasant to watch and to hear, and to think of touching. Carella and Hawes, charmed to their shoes, found themselves relaxing in her presence.

'This cheque,' Carella said, tapping the photostat. 'What was it for?'

'June's rent. I received it on the tenth of July. Claudia always paid her rent by the tenth of the month. She was a very good tenant.'

'The apartment cost seven hundred and fifty dollars a month?'

'Yes.'

'Isn't that high for an apartment?'

'Not in Stewart City,' Mrs Miller said gently. 'And this was a river-front apartment.'

'I see. I take it Miss Davis had a good job.'

'No, no, she doesn't have a job at all.'

'Then how could she afford ... ?'

'Well, she's rather well off, you know.'

'Where does she get the money, Mrs Miller?'

'Well ...' Mrs Miller shrugged. 'I really think you should ask *her*, don't you? I mean, if this is something concerning Claudia, shouldn't you ... ?'

'Mrs Miller,' Carella said, 'Claudia Davis is dead.'

'What?'

'She's ...'

'What? No. No.' She shook her head. 'Claudia? But the cheque ... I ... the cheque came only last month.' She shook her head again. 'No. No.'

'She's dead, Mrs Miller,' Carella said gently. 'She was strangled.'

The charm faltered for just an instant. Revulsion knifed the eyes of Mrs Miller, the eyelids flickered, it seemed for an instant that the pupils would turn shining and wet, that the carefully lipsticked mouth would crumble. And then something inside took over, something that demanded control, something that reminded her that a charming woman does not weep and cause her fashionable eye make-up to run.

'I'm sorry,' she said, almost in a whisper. 'I am really, really sorry. She was a nice person.'

'Can you tell us what you know about her, Mrs Miller?'

'Yes. Yes, of course.' She shook her head again, unwilling to accept the idea. 'That's terrible. That's terrible. Why, she was only a baby.'

'We figured her for thirty, Mrs Miller. Are we wrong?'

'She seemed younger, but perhaps that was because ... well, she was a rather shy person. Even when she first came here, there was an air of – well, lostness about her. Of course, that was right after her parents died, so ...'

'Where did she come from, Mrs Miller?'

'California. Santa Monica.'

Carella nodded. 'You were starting to tell us ... you said she was rather well off. Could you ... ?'

'Well, the stock, you know.'

'What stock?'

'Her parents had set up a securities trust account for her. When they died, Claudia began receiving the income from the stock. She was an only child, you know.'

'And she lived on stock dividends alone?'

'They amounted to quite a bit. Which she saved, I might add. She was a very systematic person, not at all frivolous. When she received a dividend cheque, she would endorse it and take it straight to the bank. Claudia was a very sensible girl.'

'Which bank, Mrs Miller?'

'The Highland Trust. Right down the street. On Cromwell Avenue.'

'I see,' Carella said. 'Was she dating many men? Would you know?'

'I don't think so. She kept pretty much to herself. Even after Josie came.'

Carella leaned forward. 'Josie? Who's Josie?'

'Josie Thompson. Josephine, actually. Her cousin.'

'And where did *she* come from?'

'California. They both came from California.'

'And how can we get in touch with this Josie Thompson?'

'Well, she ... Don't you know? Haven't you ... ?'

'What, Mrs Miller?'

'Why, Josie is dead. Josie passed on in June. That's why Claudia moved, I suppose. I suppose she couldn't bear the thought of living in that apartment without Josie. It *is* a little frightening, isn't it?'

'Yes,' Carella said.

DETECTIVE DIVISION SUPPLEMENTARY REPORT	SQUAD	PRECINCT	PRECINCT REPORT	DETECTIVE DIVISION REPORT NUMBER
pdcn 360 rev 25m	87	87	32-101	DD 60 R-42

NAME AND ADDRESS OF PERSON REPORTING				DATE ORIGINAL REPORT
Miller Irene (Mrs John) 13 Stewart Place S				8-4-60
SURNAME GIVEN NAME INITIALS NUMBER STREET				

DETAILS

Summary of interview with Irene (Mrs John) Miller at office of Management Enterprises Inc, address above, in re homicide Claudia Davis.

Mrs Miller states:

Claudia Davis came to this city in June of 1955, took $750-a-month apartment above address, lived there alone. Rarely seen in company of friends, male or female. Young recluse type living on substantial income of inherited securities. Parents, Mr and Mrs Carter Davis, killed on San Diego Freeway in head-on collision with station wagon, April 14 1955. LAPD confirms traffic accident, driver of other vehicle convicted for negligent operation. Mrs Miller describes girl as medium height and weight, close-cropped brunette hair, brown eyes, no scars or birthmarks she can remember, tallies with what we have on corpse. Further says Claudia Davis was quiet, unobtrusive tenant, paid rent and all service bills punctually, was gentle, sweet, plain, childlike, shy, meticulous in money matters well liked but unapproachable.

In April or May of 1959, Josie Thompson, cousin of deceased, arrived from Brentwood, California. (Routine check with Criminal Bureau Identification negative, no record. Checking now with LAPD, and FBI.) Described as slightly older than Claudia, rather different in looks and personality. 'They were like black and white,' Mrs Miller says, 'but they hit it off exceptionally well.' Josie moved into the apartment with cousin. Words used to describe relationship between two were 'like the closest of sisters' and 'really in tune', and the 'best of friends', etc. Girls did not date much, were constantly in each other's company, Josie seeming to pick up recluse habits from Claudia. Went on frequent trips together. Spent summer of '59 on Tortoise Island in the bay, returned Labor Day. Went away again at Christmas time to ski Sun Valley, and again in March this year to Kingston, Jamaica, for three weeks, returning at beginning of April. Source of income was fairly standard securities-income account. Claudia did not own the stock, but income on it was hers for as long as she lived. Trust specified that upon her death the stock and income to be turned over to UCLA (father's alma mater). In any case, Claudia was assured of a very, very substantial lifetime income (see Highland Trust bank account) and was apparently supporting Josie as well, since Mrs Miller claims neither girl worked. Brought up question of possible lesbianism, but Mrs Miller, who is knowledgeable and hip, says no, neither girl was a dike.

On June 3, Josie and Claudia left for another weekend trip. Doorman reports having helped them pack valises into trunk of Claudia's car, 1960 Cadillac convertible. Claudia did the driving. Girls did not return on Monday morning as they had indicated they would. Claudia called on Wednesday, crying

on telephone. Told Mrs Miller that Josie had had a terrible
accident and was dead. Mrs Miller remembers asking Claudia
if she could help in any way. Claudia said, quote, No,
everything's been taken care of already,

unquote.

On June 17, Mrs Miller received a letter from Claudia (letter
attached handwriting compares positive with cheques Claudia
signed) stating she could not possibly return to apartment,
not after what had happened to her cousin. She reminded Mrs
Miller lease expired on July 4, told her that she would send
cheque for June's rent before July 10. Said moving company
would pack and pick up her belongings, delivering all valuables
and documents to her, and storing rest. (see Claudia Davis'
cheque number 010, 7/14, made payable to Allora Brothers Inc.,
in payment for packing, moving and storage) Claudia Davis
never returned to the apartment. Mrs Miller had not seen her
and knew nothing of her whereabouts until we informed her of
the homicide.

DATE OF THIS REPORT

August 6

RANK	SURNAME	INITIALS	SHIELD NUMBER	COMMANDING OFFICER
Det 2/gr	Carella	S.L.	714-50-32	Det/Lt Peter Byrnes

6

The drive upstate to Triangle Lake was a particularly scenic one, and since it was August, and since Sunday was supposed to be Carella's day off, he thought he might just as well combine a little business with pleasure. So he put the top of the car down, and he packed Teddy into the front seat together with a picnic lunch and a gallon Thermos of iced coffee, and he forgot all about Claudia Davis on the drive up through the mountains. Carella found it easy to forget about almost anything when he was with his wife.

Teddy, as far as he was concerned – and his astute judgement had been backed up by many a street-corner whistle – was only the most beautiful woman in the world. He could never understand how he, a hairy, corny, ugly, stupid, clumsy cop, had managed to capture anyone as wonderful as Theodora Franklin. But capture her he had, and he sat beside her now in the open car and stole sidelong glances at her as he drove, excited as always by her very presence.

Her black hair, always wild, seemed to capture something of the wind's frenzy as it whipped about the oval of her face. Her brown eyes were partially squinted against the rush of air over the windshield. She wore a white blouse emphatically curved over a full bosom, black tapered slacks form-fitted over generous hips and good legs. She had kicked off her sandals and folded her knees against her breasts, her bare feet pressed against the glove-compartment panel. There was about her, Carella realized, a curious combination of savage and sophisticate. You never knew whether she was going to kiss you or slug you, and the uncertainty kept her eternally desirable and exciting.

Teddy watched her husband as he drove, his big-knuckled hands on the wheel of the car. She watched him not only because it gave her pleasure to watch him, but also because he was speaking. And since she could not hear, since she had been born a deaf mute, it was essential that she look at his mouth when he spoke. He did not discuss the case at all. She knew that one of the Claudia Davis cheques had been made out to the Fancher Funeral Home in Triangle Lake and she knew that Carella wanted to talk to the proprietor of the place personally. She further knew that this was very important or he wouldn't be spending his Sunday driving all the way up-state. But he had promised her he'd combine business with pleasure. This was the pleasure part of the trip, and in defer-ence to his promise and his wife, he refrained from discuss-ing the case, which was really foremost in his mind. He talked, instead, about the scenery, and their plans for the fall, and the way the twins were growing, and how pretty Teddy looked, and how she'd better button that top button of her blouse before they got out of the car, but he never once mentioned Claudia Davis until they were standing in the office of the Fancher Funeral Home and looking into the gloomy eyes of a man who called himself Barton Scoles.

Scoles was tall and thin and he wore a black suit that he had probably worn to his own confirmation back in 1912. He was so much the stereotype of a small-town undertaker that Carella almost burst out laughing when he met him. Some-how, though, the environment was not conducive to hilarity. There was a strange smell hovering over the thick rugs and the papered walls and the hanging chandeliers. It was a while before Carella recognized it as formaldehyde and then made the automatic association and, curious for a man who had stared into the eyes of death so often, suddenly felt like retching.

'Miss Davis made out a cheque to you on July fifteenth,' Carella said. 'Can you tell me what is was for?'

'Sure can,' Scoles said. 'Had to wait a long time for that cheque. She give me only a twenty-five-dollar deposit. Usually take fifty, you know. I got stuck many a time, believe me.'

'How do you mean?' Carella asked.

'People. You bury their dead, and then sometimes they don't pay you for your work. This business isn't all fun, you know. Many's the time I handled the whole funeral and the

33

service and the burial and all, and never did get paid. Makes you lose your faith in human nature.'

'But Miss Davis finally *did* pay you.'

'Oh, sure. But I can tell you I was sweating that one out. I can tell you that. After all, she was a strange gal from the city, has the funeral here, nobody comes to it but her, sitting in the chapel out there and watching the body as if someone's going to steal it away, just her and the departed. I tell you, Mr Carella ... Is that your name?'

'Yes, Carella.'

'I tell you, it was kind of spooky. Lay there two days, she did, her cousin. And then Miss Davis asked that we bury the girl right here in the local cemetery, so I done that for her, too – all on the strength of a twenty-five-dollar deposit. That's trust, Mr Carella, with a capital T.'

'When was this, Mr Scoles?'

'The girl drowned the first weekend in June,' Scoles said. 'Had no business being out on the lake so early, anyways. That water's still icy cold in June. Don't really warm up none till the latter part July. She fell over the side of the boat – she was out there rowing, you know – and that icy water probably froze her solid, or give her cramps or something, drowned her, anyways.' Scoles shook his head. 'Had no business being out on the lake so early.'

'Did you see a death certificate?'

'Yep, Dr Donneli made it out. Cause of death was drowning, all right, no question about it. We had an inquest, too, you know. The Tuesday after she drowned. They said it was accidental.'

'You said she was out rowing in a boat. Alone?'

'Yep. Her cousin, Miss Davis, was on the shore watching. Jumped in when she fell overboard, tried to reach her, but couldn't make it in time. That water's plenty cold, believe me. Ain't too warm even now, and here it is August already.'

'But it didn't seem to affect Miss Davis, did it?'

'Well, she was probably a strong swimmer. Been my experience most pretty girls are strong girls, too. I'll bet your wife here is a strong girl. She sure is a pretty one.'

Scoles smiled, and Teddy smiled, and squeezed Carella's hand.

'About the payment,' Carella said, 'for the funeral and the burial. Do you have any idea why it took Miss Davis so long to send her cheque?'

'Nope. I wrote her twice. First time was just a friendly little reminder. Second time, I made it a little stronger. Attorney friend of mine in town wrote it on his stationery; that always impresses them. Didn't get an answer either time. Finally, right out of the blue, the cheque came, payment in full. Beats me. Maybe she was affected by the death. Or maybe she's always slow paying her debts. I'm just happy the cheque came, that's all. Sometimes the live ones can give you more trouble than them who's dead, believe me.'

They strolled down to the lake together, Carella and his wife, and ate their picnic lunch on its shores. Carella was strangely silent. Teddy dangled her bare feet in the water. The water, as Scoles had promised, was very cold even though it was August. On the way back from the lake Carella said, 'Honey, would you mind if I make one more stop?'

Teddy turned her eyes to him inquisitively.

'I want to see the chief of police here.'

Teddy frowned. The question was in her eyes, and he answered it immediately.

'To find out whether or not there were any witnesses to that drowning. *Besides* Claudia Davis, I mean. From the way Scoles was talking, I get the impression that lake was pretty deserted in June.'

The chief of police was a short man with a pot belly and big feet. He kept his feet propped up on his desk all the while he spoke to Carella. Carella watched him and wondered why everybody in this damned town seemed to be on vacation from an MGM movie. A row of rifles in a locked rack was behind the chief's desk. A host of WANTED fliers covered a bulletin board to the right of the rack. The chief had a hole in the sole of his left shoe.

'Yep,' he said, 'there was a witness, all right.'

Carella felt a pang of disappointment. 'Who?' he asked.

'Fellow fishing at the lake. Saw the whole thing. Testified before the coroner's jury.'

'What'd he say?'

'Said he was fishing there when Josie Thompson took the boat out. Said Claudia Davis stayed behind, on the shore. Said Miss Thompson fell overboard and went under like a stone. Said Miss Davis jumped in the water and began swimming towards her. Didn't make it in time. That's what he said.'

'What else did he say?'

'Well, he drove Miss Davis back to town in her car. 1960 Caddy convertible, I believe. She could hardly speak. She was sobbing and mumbling and wringing her hands, oh, in a hell of a mess. Why, we had to get the whole story out of that fishing fellow. Wasn't until the next day that Miss Davis could make any kind of sense.'

'When did you hold the inquest?'

'Tuesday. Day before they buried the cousin. Coroner did the dissection on Monday. We got authorization from Miss Davis, Penal Law 2213, next of kin being charged by law with the duty of burial may authorize dissection for the sole purpose of ascertaining the cause of death.'

'And the coroner reported the cause of death as drowning?'

'That's right. Said so right before the jury.'

'Why'd you have an inquest? Did you suspect something more than accidental drowning?'

'Not necessarily. But that fellow who was fishing, well, *he* was from the city, too, you know. And for all we knew, him and Miss Davis could have been in this together, you know, shoved the cousin over the side of the boat, and then faked up a whole story, you know. They both coulda been lying in their teeth.'

'Were they?'

'Not so we could tell. You never seen anybody so grief-stricken as Miss Davis was when the fishing fellow drove her into town. Girl would have to be a hell of an actress to be-

36

have that way. Calmed down the next day, but you shoulda seen her when it happened. And at the inquest it was plain this fishing fellow had never met her before that day at the lake. Convinced the jury he had no prior knowledge of or connection with either of the two girls. Convinced me, too, for that matter.'

'What's his name?' Carella asked. 'This fishing fellow.'

'Courtenoy.'

'What did you say?'

'Courtenoy. Sidney Courtenoy.'

'Thanks,' Carella answered, and he rose suddenly. 'Come on, Teddy. I want to get back to the city.'

7

Courtenoy lived in a one-family clapboard house in River-head. He was rolling up the door of his garage when Carella and Meyer pulled into his driveway early Monday morning. He turned to look at the car curiously, one hand on the rising garage door. The door stopped, halfway up, halfway down. Carella stepped into the driveway.

'Mr Courtenoy?' he asked.

'Yes?' He stared at Carella, puzzlement on his face, the puzzlement that is always there when a perfect stranger addresses you by name. Courtenoy was a man in his late forties, wearing a cap and a badly fitted sports jacket and dark flannel slacks in the month of August. His hair was greying at the temples. He looked tired, very tired, and his weariness had nothing whatever to do with the fact that it was only seven o'clock in the morning. A lunch box was at his feet where he had apparently put it when he began rolling up the garage door. The car in the garage was a 1953 Ford.

'We're police officers,' Carella said. 'Mind if we ask you a few questions?'

'I'd like to see your badge,' Courtenoy said. Carella showed it to him. Courtenoy nodded as if he had performed a precautionary public duty. 'What are your questions?' he said. 'I'm on my way to work. Is this about that damn building permit again?'

'What building permit?'

'For extending the garage. I'm buying my son a little jalopy, don't want to leave it out on the street. Been having a hell of a time getting a building permit. Can you imagine that? All I want to do is add another twelve feet to the garage. You'd think I was trying to build a city park or something. Is that what this is about?'

From inside the house a woman's voice called, 'Who is it, Sid?'

'Nothing, nothing,' Courtenoy said impatiently. 'Nobody. Never mind, Bett.' He looked at Carella. 'My wife. You married?'

'Yes, sir, I'm married,' Carella said.

'Then you know,' Courtenoy said cryptically. 'What are your questions?'

'Ever see this before?' Carella asked. He handed a photostated copy of the cheque to Courtenoy, who looked at it briefly and handed it back.

'Sure.'

'Want to explain it, Mr Courtenoy?'

'Explain what?'

'Explain why Claudia Davis sent you a cheque for a hundred and twenty dollars.'

'As recompense,' Courtenoy said unhesitatingly.

'Oh, recompense, huh?' Meyer said. 'For what, Mr Courtenoy? For a little cock-and-bull story?'

'Huh? What are you talking about?'

'Recompense for *what*, Mr Courtenoy?'

'For missing three days' work, what the hell did you think?'

'How's that again?'

'No, what did you *think*?' Courtenoy said angrily, waving his finger at Meyer. 'What did you think it was for? Some kind of payoff or something? Is that what you thought?'

'Mr Courtenoy ...'

'I lost three days' work because of that damn inquest. I had to stay up at Triangle Lake all day Monday and Tuesday and then again on Wednesday waiting for the jury decision. I'm a bricklayer. I get five bucks an hour and I lost three days' work, eight hours a day, and so Miss Davis was good enough to send me a cheque for a hundred and twenty bucks. Now just what the hell did you think, would you mind telling me?'

'Did you know Miss Davis before that day at Triangle Lake, Mr Courtenoy?'

'Never saw her before in my life. What is this? Am I on trial here? What is this?'

From inside the house the woman's voice came again, sharply, 'Sidney! Is something wrong? Are you all right?'

'Nothing's wrong. Shut up, will you?'

There was an aggrieved silence from within the clapboard structure. Courtenoy muttered something under his breath and then turned to face the detectives again. 'You finished?' he said.

'Not quite, Mr Courtenoy. We'd like you to tell us what you saw that day at the lake.'

'What the hell for? Go read the minutes of the inquest if you're so damn interested. I've got to get to work.'

'That can wait, Mr Courtenoy.'

'Like hell it can. This job is away over in ...'

'Mr Courtenoy, we don't want to have to go all the way downtown and come back with a warrant for your arrest.'

'My *arrest*! For what? Listen, what did I ... ?'

'Sidney? Sidney, shall I call the police?' the woman shouted from inside the house.

'Oh, shut the hell up!' Courtenoy answered. 'Call the police,' he mumbled. 'I'm up to my ears in cops, and she wants to call the police. What do you want from me? I'm an honest bricklayer. I saw a girl drown. I told it just the way I saw it. Is that a crime? Why are you bothering me?'

'Just tell it again, Mr Courtenoy. Just the way you saw it.'

'She was out in the boat,' Courtenoy said, sighing. 'I was

fishing. Her cousin was on the shore. She fell over the side.'

'Josie Thompson.'

'Yes, Josie Thompson, whatever the hell her name was.'

'She was alone in the boat.'

'Yes. She was alone in the boat.'

'Go on.'

'The other one – Miss Davis – screamed and ran into the water, and began swimming towards her.' He shook his head. 'She didn't make it in time. That boat was a long way out. When she got there, the lake was still. She dove under and came up, and then dove under again, but it was too late, it was just too late. Then, as she was swimming back, I thought *she* was going to drown, too. She faltered and sank below the surface, and I waited and I thought sure she was gone. Then there was a patch of yellow that broke through the water, and I saw she was all right.'

'Why didn't you jump in to help her, Mr Courtenoy?'

'I don't know how to swim.'

'All right. What happened next?'

'She came out of the water – Miss Davis. She was exhausted and hysterical. I tried to calm her down, but she kept yelling and crying, not making any sense at all. I dragged her over to the car, and I asked her for the car keys. She didn't seem to know what I was talking about at first. "The keys!" I said, and she just stared at me. "Your car keys!" I yelled. "The keys to the car." Finally she reached in her purse and handed me the keys.'

'Go on.'

'I drove her into town. It was me who told the story to the police. She couldn't talk, all she could do was babble and scream and cry. It was a terrible thing to watch. I'd never before seen a woman so completely off her nut. We couldn't get two straight words out of her until the next day. Then she was all right. Told the police who she was, explained what I'd already told them the day before, and told them the dead girl was her cousin, Josie Thompson. They dragged the lake and got her out of the water. A shame. A real shame. Nice young girl like that.'

'What was the dead girl wearing?'

'Cotton dress. Loafers, I think. Or sandals. Little thin sweater over the dress. A cardigan.'

'Any jewellery?'

'I don't think so. No.'

'Was she carrying a purse?'

'No. Her purse was in the car with Miss Davis.'

'What was Miss Davis wearing?'

'When? The day of the drowning? Or when they pulled her cousin out of the lake?'

'Was she there then?'

'Sure. Identified the body.'

'No, I wanted to know what she was wearing on the day of the accident, Mr Courtenoy.'

'Oh, skirt and a blouse, I think. Ribbon in her hair. Loafers. I'm not sure.'

'What colour blouse? Yellow?'

'No. Blue.'

'You said yellow.'

'No, blue. I didn't say yellow.'

Carella frowned. 'I thought you said yellow earlier.' He shrugged. 'All right, what happened after the inquest?'

'Nothing much. Miss Davis thanked me for being so kind and said she would send me a cheque for the time I'd missed. I refused at first and then I thought, What the hell, I'm a hard-working man, and money doesn't grow on trees. So I gave her my address. I figured she could afford it. Driving a Caddy, and hiring a fellow to take it back to the city.'

'Why didn't she drive it back herself?'

'I don't know. I guess she was still a little shaken. Listen, that was a terrible experience. Did you ever see anyone die up close?'

'Yes,' Carella said.

From inside the house Courtenoy's wife yelled, 'Sidney, tell those men to get out of our driveway!'

'You heard her,' Courtenoy said, and finished rolling up his garage door.

8

Nobody likes Monday morning.

It was invented for hangovers. It is really not the beginning of a new week, but only the tail end of the week before. Nobody likes it, and it doesn't have to be rainy or gloomy or blue in order to provoke disaffection. It can be bright and sunny and the beginning of August. It can start with a driveway interview at seven a.m. and grow progressively worse by nine-thirty that same morning. Monday is Monday and legislation will never change its personality. Monday is Monday, and it stinks.

By nine-thirty that Monday morning, Detective Steve Carella was on the edge of total bewilderment and, like any normal person, he blamed it on Monday. He had come back to the squadroom and painstakingly gone over the pile of cheques Claudia Davis had written during the month of July, a total of twenty-five, searching them for some clue to her strangulation, studying them with the scrutiny of a typographer in a print shop. Several things seemed evident from the cheques, but nothing seemed pertinent. He could recall having said: 'I look at those cheques, I can see a life. It's like reading somebody's diary,' and he was beginning to believe he had uttered some famous last words in those two succinct sentences. For if this was the diary of Claudia Davis, it was a singularly unprovocative account that would never make the nation's bestseller lists.

Most of the cheques had been made out to clothing or department stores. Claudia, true to the species, seemed to have a penchant for shopping and a chequebook that yielded to her spending urge. Calls to the various stores represented revealed that her taste ranged through a wide variety of items. A check of sales slips showed that she had purchased during the month of July alone three baby doll nightgowns, two half slips, a trenchcoat, a wristwatch, four pairs of tapered slacks in various colours, two pairs of walking shoes, a pair of sunglasses, four bikini swimsuits, eight wash-and-wear frocks, two skirts, two cashmere sweaters, half-a-dozen bestselling novels, a large bottle of aspirin, two bottles of Dramamine, six pieces of luggage, and four boxes of cleansing tissue. The most expensive thing she had purchased was an evening gown costing $500. These purchases accounted for most of the cheques she had drawn in July. There were also cheques to a hairdresser, a florist, a shoemaker, a candy shop, and three unexplained cheques that were drawn to individuals, two men and a woman.

The first was made out to George Badueck.

The second was made out to David Oblinsky.

The third was made out to Martha Fedelson.

Someone on the squad had attacked the telephone directory and come up with addresses for two of the three. The third, Oblinsky, had an unlisted number, but a half-hour's argument with a supervisor had finally netted an address for him. The completed list was now on Carella's desk together with all the cancelled cheques. He should have begun tracking down those names, he knew, but something was still bugging him.

'Why did Courtenoy lie to me and Meyer?' he asked Cotton Hawes. 'Why did he lie about something as simple as what Claudia Davis was wearing on the day of the drowning?'

'How did he lie?'

'First he said she was wearing yellow, said he saw a patch of yellow break the surface of the lake. Then he changed it to blue. Why did he do that, Cotton?'

'I don't know.'

'And if he lied about that, why couldn't he have been lying about everything? Why couldn't he and Claudia have done in little Josie together?'

'I don't know,' Hawes said.

'Where'd that twenty thousand bucks come from, Cotton?'

'Maybe it was a stock dividend.'

'Maybe. Then why didn't she simply deposit the cheque? This was cash, Cotton, *cash*. Now where did it come from?

That's a nice piece of change. You don't pick twenty grand out of the gutter.'

'I suppose not.'

'I know where you can get twenty grand, Cotton.'

'Where?'

'From an insurance company. When someone dies.' Carella nodded once, sharply. 'I'm going to make some calls. Damnit, that money had to come from *some*place.'

He hit pay dirt on his sixth call. The man he spoke to was named Jeremiah Dodd and was a representative of the Security Insurance Corporation, Inc. He recognized Josie Thompson's name at once.

'Oh, yes,' he said. 'We settled that claim in July.'

'Who made the claim, Mr Dodd?'

'The beneficiary, of course. Just a moment. Let me get the folder on this. Will you hold on, please?'

Carella waited impatiently. Over at the insurance company on the other end of the line he could hear muted voices. A girl giggled suddenly, and he wondered who was kissing whom over by the water cooler. At last Dodd came back on the line.

'Here it is,' he said. 'Josephine Thompson. Beneficiary was her cousin, Miss Claudia Davis. Oh, yes, now it's all coming back. Yes, this is the one.'

'What one?'

'Where the girls were mutual beneficiaries.'

'What do you mean?'

'The cousins,' Dodd said. 'There were two life policies. One for Miss Davis and one for Miss Thompson. And they were mutual beneficiaries.'

'You mean Miss Davis was the beneficiary of Miss Thompson's policy and vice versa?'

'Yes, that's right.'

'That's very interesting. How large were the policies?'

'Oh, very small.'

'Well, how *small* then?'

'I believe they were both insured for twelve thousand five hundred. Just a moment; let me check. Yes, that's right.'

'And Miss Davis applied for payment on the policy after her cousin died, huh?'

'Yes. Here it is, right here. Josephine Thompson drowned at Lake Triangle on June fourth. That's right. Claudia Davis sent in the policy and the certificate of death and also a coroner's jury verdict.'

'She didn't miss a trick, did she?'

'Sir? I'm sorry, I ...'

'Did you pay her?'

'Yes. It was a perfectly legitimate claim. We began processing it at once.'

'Did you send anyone up to Lake Triangle to investigate the circumstances of Miss Thompson's death?'

'Yes, but it was merely a routine investigation. A coroner's inquest is good enough for us, Detective Carella.'

'When did you pay Miss Davis?'

'On July first.'

'You sent her a cheque for twelve thousand five hundred dollars, is that right?'

'No, sir.'

'Didn't you say ... ?'

'The policy insured her for twelve-five, that's correct. But there was a double-indemnity clause, you see, and Josephine Thompson's death was accidental. No, we had to pay the policy's limit, Detective Carella. On July first we sent Claudia Davis a cheque for twenty-five thousand dollars.'

9

There are no mysteries in police work.

Nothing fits into a carefully preconceived scheme. The high point of any given case is very often the corpse that opens the case. There is no climactic progression; suspense is for the movies. There are only people and curiously twisted motives, and small unexplained details, and coincidence, and the unexpected, and they combine to form a sequence of events, but there is no real mystery, there never is. There is only life, and sometimes death, and neither follows a rule book. Policemen hate mystery stories because they recognize in them a control that is lacking in their own very real, sometimes routine, sometimes spectacular, sometimes tedious investigation of a case. It is very nice and very clever and very convenient to have all the pieces fit together neatly. It is very kind to think of detectives as master mathematicians working on an algebraic problem whose constants are death and a victim, whose unknown is a murderer. But many of these mastermind detectives have trouble adding up the deductions on their twice-monthly paycheques. The world is full of wizards, for sure, but hardly any of them work for the city police.

There was one big mathematical discrepancy in the Claudia Davis case.

There seemed to be $5,000 unaccounted for.

Twenty-five grand had been mailed to Claudia Davis on July 1, and she presumably received the cheque after the Fourth of July holiday, cashed it someplace, and then took her money to the Seaboard Bank of America, opened a new chequing account, and rented a safe-deposit box. But her total deposit at Seaboard had been $20,000 whereas the cheque had been for $25,000, so where was the laggard five? And who had cashed the cheque for her? Mr Dodd of the Security Insurance Corporation, Inc, explained the company's rather complicated accounting system to Carella. A cheque was kept in the local office for several days after it was cashed in order to close out the policy, after which it was sent to the main office in Chicago where it sometimes stayed for several weeks until the master files were closed out. It was then sent to the company's accounting and auditing firm in San Francisco. It was Dodd's guess that the cancelled cheque had already been sent to the California accountants, and he promised to put a tracer on it at once. Carella asked him to please hurry. Someone had cashed that cheque for Claudia and, supposedly, someone also had one-fifth of the cheque's face value.

The very fact that Claudia had not taken the cheque itself to Seaboard seemed to indicate that she had something to hide. Presumably, she did not want anyone asking questions about insurance company cheques, or insurance policies, or double indemnities, or accidental drownings, or especially her cousin Josie. The cheque was a perfectly good one, and yet she had chosen to cash it *before* opening a new account. Why? And why, for that matter, had she bothered opening a new account when she had a rather well-stuffed and active account at another bank?

There are only whys in police work, but they do not add up to mystery. They add up to work, and nobody in the world likes work. The bulls of the 87th would have preferred to sit on their backsides and sip at gin-and-tonics, but the whys were there, so they put on their hats and their holsters and tried to find some becauses.

Cotton Hawes systematically interrogated each and every tenant in the rooming house where Claudia Davis had been killed. They all had alibis tighter than the closed fist of an Arabian stablekeeper. In his report to the lieutenant, Hawes expressed the belief that none of the tenants was guilty of homicide. As far as he was concerned, they were all clean.

Meyer Meyer attacked the 87th's stool pigeons. There were moneychangers galore in the precinct and the city, men who turned hot loot into cold cash – for a price. If someone had cashed a $25,000 cheque for Claudia and kept $5,000 of it during the process, couldn't that person conceivably be one of the moneychangers? He put the precinct stoolies on the ear, asked them to sound around for word of a Security Insurance Corporation cheque. The stoolies came up with nothing.

Detective Lieutenant Sam Grossman took his laboratory boys to the murder room and went over it again. And again. And again. He reported that the lock on the door was a snap lock, the kind that clicks shut automatically when the door is slammed. Whoever killed Claudia Davis could have done so without performing any locked-room gymnastics. All he had to do was close the door behind him when he left. Grossman also reported that Claudia's bed had apparently not been slept in on the night of the murder. A pair of shoes had been found at the foot of a large easy chair in the bedroom and a novel was wedged open on the arm of the chair. He suggested that Claudia had fallen asleep while reading, had awakened, and gone into the other room where she had met her murderer and her death. He had no suggestion as to just who that murderer might have been.

Steve Carella was hot and impatient and overloaded. There were other things happening in the precinct, things like burglaries and muggings and knifings and assaults and kids with summertime on their hands hitting other kids with ball bats because they didn't like the way they pronounced the word 'señor'. There were telephones jangling, and reports to be typed in triplicate, and people filing into the squadroom day and night with complaints against the citizenry of that fair city, and the Claudia Davis case was beginning to be a big fat pain in the keester. Carella wondered what it was like to be a shoemaker. And while he was wondering, he began to chase down the cheques made out to George Badueck, David Oblinsky, and Martha Fedelson.

Happily, Bert Kling had nothing whatsoever to do with the Claudia Davis case. He hadn't even discussed it with any of the men on the squad. He was a young detective and a new detective, and the things that happened in that precinct were enough to drive a guy nuts and keep him busy forty-eight hours every day, so he didn't go around sticking his nose into other people's cases. He had enough troubles of his own. One of those troubles was the line-up.

On Wednesday morning Bert Kling's name appeared on the line-up duty chart.

10

The line-up was held in the gym downtown at Headquarters on High Street. It was held four days a week, Monday to Thursday, and the purpose of the parade was to acquaint the city's detectives with the people who were committing crime, the premise being that crime is a repetitive profession and that a crook will always be a crook, and it's good to know who your adversaries are should you happen to come face to face with them on the street. Timely recognition of a thief had helped crack many a case and had, on some occasions, even saved a detective's life. So the line-up was a pretty valuable in-group custom. This didn't mean that detectives enjoyed the trip downtown. They drew line-up perhaps once every two weeks and, often as not, line-up duty fell on their day off, and nobody appreciated rubbing elbows with criminals on his day off.

The line-up that Wednesday morning followed the classic pattern of all line-ups. The detectives sat in the gymnasium on folding chairs, and the chief of detectives sat behind a high podium at the back of the gym. The green shades were drawn, and the stage illuminated, and the offenders who'd been arrested the day before were marched before the assembled bulls while the chief read off the charges and handled the interrogation. The pattern was a simple one. The arresting officer, uniformed or plainclothes, would join the chief at the rear of the gym when his arrest came up. The chief would read off the felon's name, and then the section of the city in which he'd been arrested, and then a number. He would say, for example, 'Jones, John, Riverhead, three.' The 'three' would simply indicate that this was the third arrest in Riverhead that day. Only felonies and special types of misdemeanours were handled at the line-up, so this narrowed the list of performers on any given day. Following the case number, the chief would read off the offence, and then say either 'Statement' or 'No statement', telling the assembled cops that the thief either had or had not said anything when they'd put the collar on him. If there had been a statement, the chief would limit his questions to rather general topics since he didn't want to lead the felon into saying anything that might contradict his usually incriminating initial statement, words that could be used against him in court. If there had been *no* statement, the chief would pull out all the stops. He was generally armed with whatever police records were available on the man who stood under the blinding lights, and it was the smart thief who understood the purpose of the line-up and who knew he was not bound to answer a goddamned thing they asked him. The chief of detectives was something like a deadly earnest Mike Wallace, but the stakes were slightly higher here because this involved something a little more important than a novelist plugging his new book or a senator explaining the stand he had taken on a farm bill. These were truly 'interviews in depth', and the booby prize was very often a long stretch up the river in a cosy one-windowed room.

The line-up bored the hell out of Kling. It always did. It was like seeing a stage show for the hundredth time. Every now and then somebody stopped the show with a really good routine. But usually it was the same old song and dance. It wasn't any different that Wednesday. By the time the eighth offender had been paraded and subjected to the chief's bludgeoning interrogation, Kling was beginning to doze. The detective sitting next to him nudged him gently in the ribs.

'... Reynolds, Ralph,' the chief was saying, 'Isola, four. Caught burgling an apartment on North Third. No statement. How about it, Ralph?'

'How about what?'

'You do this sort of thing often?'

'What sort of thing?'

'Burglary.'

'I'm no burglar,' Reynolds said.

'I've got his B-sheet here,' the chief said. 'Arrested for burglary in 1948, witness withdrew her testimony, claimed she had mistakenly identified him. Arrested again for burglary in 1952, convicted for Burglary One, sentenced to ten at Castleview, paroled in '58 on good behaviour. You're back at the old stand, huh, Ralph?'

'No, not me. I've been straight ever since I got out.'

'Then what were you doing in that apartment during the middle of the night?'

'I was a little drunk. I must have walked into the wrong building.'

'What do you mean?'

'I thought it was my apartment.'

'Where do you live, Ralph?'

'Oh ... uh ... well ...'

'Come on, Ralph.'

'Well, I live on South Fifth.'

'And the apartment you were in last night is on North Third. You must have been pretty drunk to wander that far off course.'

'Yeah, I guess I was pretty drunk.'

'Woman in that apartment said you hit her when she woke up. Is that true, Ralph?'

'No. No, hey, I never hit her.'

'She says so, Ralph.'

'Well, she's mistaken.'

'Well, now, a doctor's report says somebody clipped her on the jaw, Ralph, now how about that?'

'Well, maybe.'

'Yes or no?'

'Well, maybe when she started screaming she got me nervous. I mean, you know, I thought it was my apartment and all.'

'Ralph, you were burgling that apartment. How about telling us the truth?'

'No, I got in there by mistake.'

'How'd you get in?'

'The door was open.'

'In the middle of the night, huh? The door was open?'

'Yeah.'

'You sure you didn't pick the lock or something, huh?'

'No, no. Why would I do that? I thought it was my apartment.'

'Ralph, what were you doing with burglar's tools?'

'Who? Who me? Those weren't burglar's tools.'

'Then what were they? You had a glass cutter, and a bunch of jimmies, and some punches, and a drill and bits, and three celluloid strips, and some lock-picking tools, and eight skeleton keys. Those sound like burglar's tools to me, Ralph.'

'No. I'm a carpenter.'

'Yeah, you're a carpenter all right, Ralph. We searched your apartment, Ralph, and found a couple of things we're curious about. Do you always keep sixteen wristwatches and four typewriters and twelve bracelets and eight rings and a mink stole and three sets of silverware, Ralph?'

'Yeah. I'm a collector.'

'Of other people's things. We also found four hundred dollars in American currency and five thousand dollars in French francs. Where'd you get that money, Ralph?'

'Which?'

'Whichever you feel like telling us about.'

'Well, the US stuff I ... I won at the track. And the other, well, a Frenchman owed me some gold, and so he paid me in francs. That's all.'

'We're checking our stolen-goods list right this minute, Ralph.'

'So check!' Reynolds said, suddenly angry. 'What the hell do you want from me? Work for your goddamn living! You

want it all on a platter! Like fun! I told you everything I'm
gonna ...'

'Get him out of here,' the chief said. 'Next, Blake, Donald,
Bethtown, two. Attempted rape. No statement ...'

Bert Kling made himself comfortable on the folding chair
and began to doze again.

11

The cheque made out to George Badueck was numbered
018. It was a small cheque, five dollars. It did not seem very
important to Carella, but it was one of the unexplained three,
and he decided to give it a whirl.

Badueck, as it turned out, was a photographer. His shop
was directly across the street from the County Court Building in Isola. A sign in his window advised that he took photo-
graphs for chauffeurs' licences, hunting licences, passports,
taxicab permits, pistol permits, and the like. The shop was
small and crowded. Badueck fitted into the shop like a beetle
in an ant trap. He was a huge man with thick, unruly black
hair and the smell of developing fluid on him.

'Who remembers?' he said. 'I get millions of people in
here every day of the week. They pay me in cash, they pay
me with cheques, they're ugly, they're pretty, they're skinny,
they're fat, they all look the same on the pictures I take.
Lousy. They all look like I'm photographing them for you
guys. You never see any of these official-type pictures? Man,
they look like mug shots, all of them. So who remembers this
... what's her name? Claudia Davis, yeah. Another face,
that's all. Another mug shot. Why? Is the cheque bad or
something?'

'No, it's a good cheque.'

'So what's the fuss?'

'No fuss,' Carella said. 'Thanks a lot.'

He sighed and went out into the August heat. The County Court Building across the street was white and Gothic in the sunshine. He wiped a handkerchief across his forehead and thought, *Another face, that's all.* Sighing, he crossed the street and entered the building. It was cool in the high vaulted corridors. He consulted the directory and went up to the Bureau of Motor Vehicles first. He asked the clerk there if anyone named Claudia Davis had applied for a licence requiring a photograph.

'We only require pictures on chauffeurs' licences,' the clerk said.

'Well, would you check?' Carella asked.

'Sure. Might take a few minutes, though. Would you have a seat?'

Carella sat. It was very cool. It felt like October. He looked at his watch. It was almost time for lunch, and he was getting hungry. The clerk came back and motioned him over.

'We've got a Claudia Davis listed,' he said, 'but she's already got a licence, and she didn't apply for a new one.'

'What kind of licence?'

'Operator's.'

'When does it expire?'

'Next September.'

'And she hasn't applied for anything needing a photo?'

'Nope. Sorry.'

'That's all right. Thanks,' Carella said.

He went out into the corridor again. He hardly thought it likely that Claudia Davis had applied for a permit to own or operate a taxicab, so he skipped the Hack Bureau and went upstairs to Pistol Permits. The woman he spoke to there was very kind and very efficient. She checked her files and told him that no one named Claudia Davis had ever applied for either a carry or a premises pistol permit. Carella thanked her and went into the hall again. He was very hungry. His stomach was beginning to growl. He debated having lunch and then returning and decided, *Hell, I'd better get it done now.*

The man behind the counter in the Passport Bureau was old and thin and he wore a green eyeshade. Carella asked his question, and the old man went to his files and creakingly returned to the window.

'That's right,' he said.

'What's right?'

'She did. Claudia Davis. She applied for a passport.'

'When?'

The old man checked the slip of paper in his trembling hands. 'July twentieth,' he said.

'Did you give it to her?'

'We accepted her application, sure. Isn't us who issues the passports. We've got to send the application on to Washington.'

'But you did accept it?'

'Sure, why not? Had all the necessary stuff. Why shouldn't we accept it?'

'What was the necessary stuff?'

'Two photos, proof of citizenship, filled-out application, and cash.'

'What did she show as proof of citizenship?'

'Her birth certificate.'

'Where was she born?'

'California.'

'She paid you in cash?'

'That's right.'

'Not a cheque?'

'Nope. She started to write a cheque, but the blamed pen was on the blink. We use ballpoints, you know, and it gave out after she filled in the application. So she paid me in cash. It's not all that much money, you know.'

'I see. Thank you,' Carella said.

'Not at all,' the old man replied, and he creaked back to his files to replace the record on Claudia Davis.

The cheque was numbered 007, and it was dated July twelfth,

and it was made out to a woman named Martha Fedelson.

Miss Fedelson adjusted her pince-nez and looked at the cheque. Then she moved some papers aside on the small desk in the cluttered office, and put the cheque down, and leaned closer to it, and studied it again.

'Yes,' she said, 'that cheque was made out to me. Claudia Davis wrote it right in this office.' Miss Fedelson smiled. 'If you can call it an office. Desk space and a telephone. But then, I'm just starting, you know.'

'How long have you been a travel agent, Miss Fedelson?'

'Six months now. It's very exciting work.'

'Had you ever booked a trip for Miss Davis before?'

'No. This was the first time.'

'Did someone refer her to you?'

'No. She picked my name out of the phone book.'

'And asked you to arrange this trip for her, is that right?'

'Yes.'

'And this cheque? What's it for?'

'Her airline tickets, and deposits at several hotels.'

'Hotels *where*?'

'In Paris and Dijon. And then another in Lausanne, Switzerland.'

'She was going to Europe?'

'Yes. From Lausanne she was heading to the Italian Riviera. I was working on that for her, too. Getting transportation and the hotels, you know.'

'When did she plan to leave?'

'September first.'

'Well, that explains the luggage and the clothes,' Carella said aloud.

'I'm sorry,' Miss Fedelson said, and she smiled and raised her eyebrows.

'Nothing, nothing,' Carella said. 'What was your impression of Miss Davis?'

'Oh, that's hard to say. She was only here once, you understand.' Miss Fedelson thought for a moment, and then said, 'I suppose she *could* have been a pretty girl if she tried, but she wasn't trying. Her hair was short and dark, and she seemed rather – well, withdrawn, I guess. She didn't take her sunglasses off all the while she was here. I suppose you would call her shy. Or frightened. I don't know.' Miss Fedelson smiled again. 'Have I helped you any?'

'Well, now we know she was going abroad,' Carella said.

'September is a good time to go,' Miss Fedelson answered. 'In September the tourists have all gone home.' There was a wistful sound to her voice. Carella thanked her for her time and left the small office with its travel folders on the cluttered desk top.

12

He was running out of cheques and running out of ideas. Everything seemed to point towards a girl in flight, a girl in hiding, but what was there to hide, what was there to run from? Josie Thompson had been in that boat alone. The coroner's jury had labelled it accidental drowning. The insurance company hadn't contested Claudia's claim, and they'd given her a legitimate cheque that she could have cashed anywhere in the world. And yet there *was* hiding, and there *was* flight – and he couldn't understand why.

He took the list of remaining cheques from his pocket. The girl's shoemaker, the girl's hairdresser, a florist, a candy shop. None of them truly important. And the remaining cheque made out to an individual, the cheque numbered 006 and dated July eleventh, and written to a man named David Oblinsky in the amount of $45.75. Carella had his lunch at two-thirty and then went downtown. He found Oblinsky in a diner near the bus terminal. Oblinsky was sitting on one of the counter stools, and he was drinking a cup of coffee. He asked Carella to join him, and Carella did.

'You traced me through that cheque, huh?' he said. 'The phone company gave you my number and my address, huh? I'm unlisted, you know. They ain't supposed to give out my number.'

'Well, they made a special concession because it was police business.'

'Yeah, well, suppose the cops called and asked for Marlon Brando's number? You think they'd give it out? Like hell they would. I don't like that. No, sir, I don't like it one damn bit.'

'What do you do, Mr Oblinsky? Is there a reason for the unlisted number?'

'I drive a cab is what I do. Sure there's a reason. It's classy to have an unlisted number. Didn't you know that?'

Carella smiled. 'No, I didn't.'

'Sure, it is.'

'Why did Claudia Davis give you this cheque?' Carella asked.

'Well, I work for a cab company here in this city, you see. But usually on weekends or on my day off I use my own car and I take people on long trips, you know what I mean? Like to the country, or the mountains, or the beach, wherever they want to go. I don't care. I'll take them wherever they want to go.'

'I see.'

'Sure. So in June sometime, the beginning of June it was, I get a call from this guy I know up at Triangle Lake, he tells me there's a rich broad there who needs somebody to drive her Caddy back to the city for her. He said it was worth thirty bucks if I was willing to take the train up and the heap back. I told him, no sir, I wanted forty-five or it was no deal. I knew I had him over a barrel, you understand? He'd already told me he checked with the local hicks and none of them felt like making the ride. So he said he would talk it over with her and get back to me. Well, he called again ... you know, it burns me up about the phone company. They ain't supposed to give out my number like that. Suppose it was Marilyn Monroe? You think they'd give out her number? I'm gonna raise a stink about this, believe me.'

'What happened when he called you back?'

'Well, he said she was willing to pay forty-five, but like could I wait until July sometime when she would send me a cheque because she was a little short at the moment. So I figured what the hell, am I going to get stiffed by a dame who's driving a 1960 Caddy? I figured I could trust her until July. But I also told him, if that was the case, then I also wanted her to pay the tolls on the way back, which I don't ordinarily ask my customers to do. That's what the seventy-five cents was for. The tolls.'

'So you took the train up there and then drove Miss Davis and the Cadillac back to the city, is that right?'

'Yeah.'

'I suppose she was pretty distraught on the trip home.'

'Huh?'

'You know. Not too coherent.'

'Huh?'

'Broken up. Crying. Hysterical,' Carella said.

'No. No, she was okay.'

'Well, what I mean is ...' Carella hesitated. 'I assumed she wasn't capable of driving the car back herself.'

'Yeah, that's right. That's why she hired me.'

'Well, then ...'

'But not because she was broken up or anything.'

'Then why?' Carella frowned. 'Was there a lot of luggage? Did she need your help with that?'

'Yeah, sure. Both hers and her cousin's. Her cousin drowned, you know.'

'Yes. I know that.'

'But anybody coulda helped her with her luggage,' Oblinsky said. 'No, that wasn't why she hired me. She really *needed* me, mister.'

'Why?'

'Why? Because she don't know how to drive, that's why.'

Carella stared at him. 'You're wrong,' he said.

'Oh, no,' Oblinsky said. 'She can't drive, believe me. While I was putting the luggage in the trunk, I asked her to start the car, and she didn't even know how to do that. Hey, you think I ought to raise a fuss with the phone company?'

'I don't know,' Carella said, rising suddenly. All at once the cheque made out to Claudia Davis' hairdresser seemed terribly important to him. He had almost run out of cheques, but all at once he had an idea.

13

The hairdresser's salon was on South Twenty-third, just off Jefferson Avenue. A green canopy covered the sidewalk outside the salon. The words ARTURO MANFREDI, INC, were lettered discreetly in white on the canopy. A glass plaque in the window repeated the name of the establishment and added, for the benefit of those who did not read either *Vogue* or *Harper's Bazaar*, that there were two branches of the shop, one here in Isola and another in 'Nassau, the Bahamas'. Beneath that, in smaller, more modest letters, were the words 'Internationally Renowned'. Carella and Hawes went into the shop at four-thirty in the afternoon. Two meticulously coiffed and manicured women were sitting in the small reception room, their expensively sleek legs crossed, apparently awaiting either their chauffeurs, their husbands, or their lovers. They both looked up expectantly when the detectives entered, expressed mild disappointment by only slightly raising newly plucked eyebrows, and went back to reading their fashion magazines. Carella and Hawes walked to the desk. The girl behind the desk was a blonde with a brilliant shellacked look and an English finishing school voice.

'Yes?' she said. 'May I help you?'

She lost a tiny trace of her poise when Carella flashed his

buzzer. She read the raised lettering on the shield, glanced at the photo on the plastic-encased ID card, quickly regained her polished calm, and said coolly and unemotionally, 'Yes, what can I do for you?'

'We wonder if you can tell us anything about the girl who wrote this cheque?' Carella said. He reached into his jacket pocket, took out a folded photostat of the cheque, unfolded it, and put it on the desk before the blonde. The blonde looked at it casually.

'What is the name?' she asked. 'I can't make it out.'

'Claudia Davis.'

'D-A-V-I-S?'

'Yes.'

'I don't recognize the name,' the blonde said. 'She's not one of our regular customers.'

'But she did make out a cheque to your salon,' Carella said. 'She wrote this on July seventh. Would you please check your records and find out why she was here and who took care of her?'

'I'm sorry,' the blonde said.

'What?'

'I'm sorry, but we close at five o'clock, and this is the busiest time of the day for us. I'm sure you can understand that. If you'd care to come back a little later . . .'

'No, we wouldn't care to come back a little later,' Carella said. 'Because if we came back a little later, it would be with a search warrant and possibly a warrant for the seizure of your books, and sometimes that can cause a little commotion among the gossip columnists, and that kind of commotion might add to your international renown a little bit. We've had a long day, miss, and this is important, so how about it?'

'Of course. We're always delighted to cooperate with the police,' the blonde said frigidly. 'Especially when they're so well mannered.'

'Yes, we're all of that,' Carella answered.

'Yes. July seventh, did you say?'

'July seventh.'

The blonde left the desk and went into the back of the

61

salon. A brunette came out front and said, 'Has Miss Marie left for the evening?'

'Who's Miss Marie?' Hawes asked.

'The blonde girl.'

'No. She's getting something for us.'

'That white streak is very attractive,' the brunette said. 'I'm Miss Olga.'

'How do you do.'

'Fine, thank you,' Miss Olga said. 'When she comes back, would you tell her there's something wrong with one of the dryers on the third floor?'

'Yes, I will,' Hawes said.

Miss Olga smiled, waved, and vanished into the rear of the salon again. Miss Marie reappeared not a moment later. She looked at Carella and said, 'A Miss Claudia Davis was here on July seventh. Mr Sam worked on her. Would you like to talk to him?'

'Yes, we would.'

'Then follow me, please,' she said curtly.

They followed her into the back of the salon past women who sat with crossed legs, wearing smocks, their heads in hair dryers.

'Oh, by the way,' Hawes said, 'Miss Olga said to tell you there's something wrong with one of the third-floor dryers.'

'Thank you,' Miss Marie said.

Hawes felt particularly clumsy in this world of women's machines. There was an air of delicate efficiency about the place, and Hawes – six feet two inches tall in his bare soles, weighing in at a hundred and ninety pounds – was certain he would knock over a bottle of nail polish or a pail of hair rinse. As they entered the second-floor salon, as he looked down that long line of humming space helmets at women with crossed legs and what looked like barbers' aprons covering their nylon slips, he became aware of a new phenomenon. The women were slowly turning their heads inside the dryers to look at the white streak over his left temple. He suddenly felt like a horse's ass. For whereas the streak was the legitimate result of a knifing – they had shaved his red hair to get at the wound, and it had grown back this way – he realized all at once that many of these women had shelled out hard-earned dollars to simulate identical white streaks in their own hair, and he no longer felt like a cop making a business call. Instead, he felt like a customer who had come to have his goddamned streak touched up a little.

'This is Mr Sam,' Miss Marie said, and Hawes turned to see Carella shaking hands with a rather elongated man. The man wasn't particularly tall, he was simply elongated. He gave the impression of being seen from the side seats in a movie theatre, stretched out of true proportion, curiously two-dimensional. He wore a white smock, and there were three narrow combs in the breast pocket. He carried a pair of scissors in one thin, sensitive-looking hand.

'How do you do?' he said to Carella, and he executed a half-bow, European in origin, American in execution. He turned to Hawes, took his hand, shook it, and again said, 'How do you do?'

'They're from the police,' Miss Marie said briskly, releasing Mr Sam from any obligation to be polite, and then left the men alone.

'A woman named Claudia Davis was here on July seventh,' Carella said. 'Apparently she had her hair done by you. Can you tell us what you remember about her?'

'Miss Davis, Miss Davis,' Mr Sam said, touching his high forehead in an attempt at visual shorthand, trying to convey the concept of thought without having to do the accompanying brainwork. 'Let me see, Miss Davis, Miss Davis.'

'Yes.'

'Yes, Miss Davis. A very pretty blonde.'

'No,' Carella said. He shook his head. 'A brunette. You're thinking of the wrong person.'

'No, I'm thinking of the right person,' Mr Sam said. He tapped his temple with one extended forefinger, another piece of visual abbreviation. 'I remember. Claudia Davis. A blonde.'

'A brunette,' Carella insisted, and he kept watching Mr Sam.

'When she left. But when she came, a blonde.'

'What?' Hawes said.

'She was a blonde, a very pretty, natural blonde. It is rare. Natural blondness, I mean. I couldn't understand why she wanted to change the colour.'

'You dyed her hair?' Hawes asked.

'That is correct.'

'Did she say *why* she wanted to be a brunette?'

'No, sir. I argued with her. I said, "You have *beau*tiful hair, I can do *mar*-vellous things with this hair of yours. You are a *blonde*, my dear, there are drab women who come in here every day of the week and *beg* to be turned into blondes." No. She would not listen. I dyed it for her.' Mr Sam seemed to become offended by the idea all over again. He looked at the detectives as if they had been responsible for the stubbornness of Claudia Davis.

'What else did you do for her, Mr Sam?' Carella asked.

'The dye, a cut, and a set. And I believe one of the girls gave her a facial and a manicure.'

'What do you mean by a cut? Was her hair long when she came here?'

'Yes, beautiful long blonde hair. She wanted it cut. I cut it.' Mr Sam shook his head. 'A pity. She looked terrible. I don't usually say this about someone I work on, but she walked out of here looking terrible. You would hardly recognize her as the same pretty blonde who came in not three hours before.'

'Maybe that was the idea,' Carella said.

'I beg your pardon?'

'Forget it. Thank you, Mr Sam. We know you're busy.'

In the street outside Hawes said, 'You knew before we went in there, didn't you, Mr Steve?'

'I suspected, Mr Cotton, I suspected. Come on, let's get back to the squad.'

14

They kicked it around like a bunch of advertising executives. They sat in Lieutenant Byrnes' office and tried to find out how the cookie crumbled and which way the Tootsie rolled. They were just throwing out a life preserver to see if anyone grabbed at it, that's all. What they were doing, you see, was running up the flag to see if anyone saluted, that's all. The lieutenant's office was a four-windowed office because he was top man in this particular combine. It was a very elegant office. It had an electric fan all its own, and a big wide desk. It got cross ventilation from the street. It was really very pleasant. Well, to tell the truth, it was a pretty ratty office in which to be holding a top-level meeting, but it was the best the precinct had to offer. And after a while you got used to the chipping paint and the soiled walls and the bad lighting and the stench of urine from the men's room down the hall. Peter Byrnes didn't work for BBD & O. He worked for the city. Somehow, there was a difference.

'I just put in a call to Irene Miller,' Carella said. 'I asked her to describe Claudia Davis to me, and she went through it all over again. Short dark hair, shy, plain. Then I asked her to describe the cousin, Josie Thompson.' Carella nodded glumly. 'Guess what?'

'A pretty girl,' Hawes said. 'A pretty girl with long blonde hair.'

'Sure. Why, Mrs Miller practically spelled it out the first time we talked to her. It's all there in the report. She said they were like black and white in looks and personality. Black and white, sure. A brunette and a goddamn blonde!'

'That explains the yellow,' Hawes said.

'What yellow?'

'Courtenoy. He said he saw a patch of yellow breaking the surface. He wasn't talking about her clothes, Steve. He was talking about her *hair*.'

'It explains a lot of things,' Carella said. 'It explains why shy Claudia Davis was preparing for her European trip by purchasing baby doll nightgowns and bikini bathing suits. And it explains why the undertaker up there referred to Claudia as a pretty girl. And it explains why our necropsy report said she was thirty when everybody talked about her as if she were much younger.'

'The girl who drowned wasn't Josie, huh?' Meyer said. 'You figure she was Claudia.'

'Damn right I figure she was Claudia.'

'And you figure she cut her hair afterwards, and dyed it, and took her cousin's name, and tried to pass as her cousin until she could get out of the country, huh?' Meyer said.

'Why?' Byrnes said. He was a compact man with a compact bullet head and a chunky economical body. He did not like to waste time or words.

'Because the trust income was in Claudia's name. Because Josie didn't have a dime of her own.'

'She could have collected on her cousin's insurance policy,' Meyer said.

'Sure, but that would have been the end of it. The trust called for those stocks to be turned over to UCLA if Claudia died. A college, for God's sake! How do you suppose Josie felt about that? Look, I'm not trying to hang a homicide on her. I just think she took advantage of a damn good situation. Claudia was in that boat alone. When she fell over the side, Josie really tried to rescue her, no question about it. But she missed, and Claudia drowned. Okay. Josie went all to pieces, couldn't talk straight, crying, sobbing, real hysterical woman, we've seen them before. But came the dawn. And with the dawn, Josie began thinking. They were away from the city, strangers in a strange town. Claudia had drowned but no one *knew* that she was Claudia. No one but Josie. She had no identification on her, remember? Her purse was in the car. Okay. If Josie identified her cousin correctly, she'd collect twenty-five grand on the insurance policy, and then all that stock would be turned over to the college, and that would be the end of the gravy train. But suppose, just suppose Josie told the police the girl in the lake was Josie Thompson?' Suppose she said, "I, Claudia Davis, tell you that girl who drowned is my cousin, Josie Thompson"?'

Hawes nodded. 'Then she'd still collect on an insurance policy, and also fall heir to those fat security dividends coming in.'

'Right. What does it take to cash a dividend cheque? A bank account, that's all. A bank account with an established signature. So all she had to do was open one, sign her name as Claudia Davis, and then endorse every dividend cheque that came in exactly the same way.'

'Which explains the new account,' Meyer said. 'She couldn't use Claudia's old account because the bank undoubtedly knew both Claudia *and* her signature. So Josie had to forfeit the sixty grand at Highland Trust and start from scratch.'

'And while she was building a new identity and a new fortune,' Hawes said, 'just to make sure Claudia's few friends forgot all about her, Josie was running off to Europe. She may have planned to stay there for years.'

'It all ties in,' Carella said. 'Claudia had a driver's licence. She was the one who drove the car away from Stewart City. But Josie had to hire a chauffeur to take her back.'

'And would Claudia, who was so meticulous about money matters, have kept so many people waiting for payment?' Hawes said. 'No, sir. That was Josie. And Josie was broke, Josie was waiting for that insurance policy to pay off so she could settle those debts and get the hell out of the country.'

'Well, I admit it adds up,' Meyer said.

Peter Byrnes never wasted words. 'Who cashed that twenty-five-thousand-dollar cheque for Josie?' he said.

There was silence in the room.

'Who's got that missing five grand?' he said.

There was another silence.

'Who *killed* Josie?' he said.

15

Jeremiah Dodd of the Security Insurance Corporation, Inc., did not call until two days later. He asked to speak to Detective Carella, and when he got him on the phone, he said, 'Mr Carella, I've just heard from San Francisco on that cheque.'

'What cheque?' Carella asked. He had been interrogating a witness to a knifing in a grocery store on Culver Avenue. The Claudia Davis or rather the Josie Thompson case was not quite yet in the Open File, but it was ready to be dumped there, and was truly the farthest thing from Carella's mind at the moment.

'The cheque that was paid to Claudia Davis,' Dodd said.

'Oh, yes. Who cashed it?'

'Well, there are two endorsements on the back. One was made by Claudia Davis, of course. The other was made by an outfit called Leslie Summers, Inc. It's a regular company stamp marked "For Deposit Only" and signed by one of the officers.'

'Have you any idea what sort of a company that is?' Carella asked.

'Yes,' Dodd said. 'They handle foreign exchange.'

'Thank you,' Carella said.

He went there with Bert Kling later that afternoon. He went with Kling completely by chance and only because Kling was heading downtown to buy his mother a birthday gift and offered Carella a ride. When they parked the car, Kling asked, 'How long will this take, Steve?'

'Few minutes, I guess.'

'Want to meet me back here?'

'Well, I'll be at 720 Hall, Leslie Summers, Inc. If you're through before me, come on over.'

'Okay, I'll see you,' Kling said.

They parted on Hall Avenue without shaking hands. Carella found the street-level office of Leslie Summers, Inc., and walked in. A counter ran the length of the room, and there were several girls behind it. One of the girls was speaking to a customer in French and another was talking Italian to a man who wanted lire in exchange for dollars. A board behind the desk quoted the current exchange rate for countries all over the world. Carella got in line and waited. When he reached the counter, the girl who'd been speaking French said, 'Yes, sir?'

'I'm a detective,' Carella said. He opened his wallet to where his shield was pinned to the leather. 'You cashed a cheque for Miss Claudia Davis sometime in July. An insurance-company cheque for twenty-five thousand dollars. Would you happen to remember it?'

'No, sir, I don't think I handled it.'

'Would you check around and see who did, please?'

The girl held a brief consultation with the other girls, and then walked to a desk behind which sat a corpulent, balding man with a razor-thin moustache. They talked with each other for a full five minutes. The man kept waving his hands. The girl kept trying to explain about the insurance-company cheque. The bell over the front door sounded. Bert Kling came in, looked around, saw Carella, and joined him at the counter.

'All done?' Carella asked.

'Yeah, I bought her a charm for her bracelet. How about you?'

'They're holding a summit meeting,' Carella said.

The fat man waddled over to the counter. 'What is the trouble?' he asked Carella.

'No trouble. Did you cash a cheque for twenty-five thousand dollars?'

'Yes. Is the cheque no good?'

'It's a good cheque.'

'It looked like a good cheque. It was an insurance-company cheque. The young lady waited while we called the company. They said it was bona fide and we should accept it. Was it a bad cheque?'

'No, no, it was fine.'

'She had identification. It all seemed very proper.'

'What did she show you?'

'A driver's licence or a passport is what we usually require. But she had neither. We accepted her birth certificate. After all, we *did* call the company. Is the cheque no good?'

'It's fine. But the cheque was for twenty-five thousand, and we're trying to find out what happened to five thousand of ...'

'Oh, yes. The francs.'

'What?'

'She bought five thousand dollars' worth of French francs,' the fat man said. 'She was going abroad?'

'Yes, she was going abroad,' Carella said. He sighed heavily. 'Well, that's that, I guess.'

'It all seemed very proper,' the fat man insisted.

'Oh, it was, it was. Thank you. Come on, Bert.'

They walked down Hall Avenue in silence.

'Beats me,' Carella said.

'What's that, Steve?'

'This case.' He sighed again. 'Oh, what the hell!'

'Yeah, let's get some coffee. What was all that business about the francs?'

'She bought five thousand dollars' worth of francs,' Carella said.

'The French are getting a big play lately, huh?' Kling said, smiling. 'Here's a place. This look okay?'

'Yeah, fine.' Carella pulled open the door of the luncheonette. 'What do you mean, Bert?'

'With the francs.'

'What about them?'

'The exchange rate must be very good.'

'I don't get you.'

'You know. All those francs kicking around.'

'Bert, what the hell are you talking about?'

'Weren't you with me? Last Wednesday?'

'With you where?'

'The line-up. I thought you were with me.'

'No, I wasn't,' Carella said tiredly.

'Oh, well, that's why.'

'That's why what? Bert, for the love of ...'

'That's why you don't remember him.'

'Who?'

'The punk they brought in on that burglary pickup. They found five grand in French francs in his apartment.'

Carella felt as if he'd just been hit by a truck.

16

It had been crazy from the beginning. Some of them are like that. The girl had looked black, but she was really white. They thought she was Claudia Davis, but she was Josie Thompson. And they had been looking for a murderer when all there happened to be was a burglar.

They brought him up from his cell where he was awaiting trial for Burglary One. He came up in an elevator with a police escort. The police van had dropped him off at the side door of the Criminal Courts Building, and he had entered the corridor under guard and been marched down through the connecting tunnel and into the building that housed the district attorney's office, and then taken into the elevator. The door of the elevator opened into a tiny room upstairs. The other door of the room was locked from the outside and a sign on it read NO ADMITTANCE. The patrolman who'd brought Ralph Reynolds up to the interrogation room stood with his back against the elevator door all the while the detectives talked to him, and his right hand was on the butt of his Police Special.

'I never heard of her,' Reynolds said.

'Claudia Davis,' Carella said. 'Or Josie Thompson. Take your choice.'

'I don't know either one of them. What the hell *is* this? You got me on a burglary rap, now you try to pull in everything was ever done in this city?'

'Who said anything was done, Reynolds?'

'If nothing was done, why'd you drag me up here?'

'They found five thousand bucks in French francs in your pad, Reynolds. Where'd you get it?'

'Who wants to know?'

'Don't get snotty, Reynolds! Where'd you get that money?'

'A guy owed it to me. He paid me in francs. He was a French guy.'

'What's his name?'

'I can't remember.'

'You'd better start trying.'

'Pierre something.'

'Pierre what?' Meyer said.

'Pierre La Salle, something like that. I didn't know him too good.'

'But you lent him five grand, huh?'

'Yeah.'

'What were you doing on the night of August first?'

'Why? What happened on August first?'

'You tell us.'

'I don't know what I was doing.'

'Were you working?'

'I'm unemployed.'

'You know what we mean!'

'No. What do you mean?'

'Were you breaking into apartments?'

'No.'

'Speak up! Yes or no?'

'I said no.'

'He's lying, Steve,' Meyer said.

'Sure he is.'

'Yeah, sure I am. Look, cop, you got nothing on me but Burglary One, if that. And that you gotta prove in court. So stop trying to hang anything else on me. You ain't got a chance.'

'Not unless those prints check out,' Carella said quickly.

'What prints?'

'The prints we found on the dead girl's throat,' Carella lied.

'I was wearing ... !'

The small room went as still as death.

Reynolds sighed heavily. He looked at the floor.

'You want to tell us?'

'No,' he said. 'Go to hell.'

He finally told them. After twelve hours of repeated questioning he finally broke down. He hadn't meant to kill her, he said. He didn't even know anybody was in the apartment. He had looked in the bedroom, and the bed was empty. He hadn't seen her asleep in one of the chairs, fully dressed. He had found the French money in a big jar on one of the shelves over the sink. He had taken the money and then accidentally dropped the jar, and she woke up and came into the room and saw him and began screaming. So he grabbed her by the throat. He only meant to shut her up. But she kept struggling. She was very strong. He kept holding on, but only to shut her up. She kept struggling, so he had to hold on. She kept struggling as if ... as if he'd really been trying to kill her, as if she didn't want to lose her life. But that was manslaughter wasn't it? He wasn't trying to kill her. That wasn't homicide, was it?

'I didn't mean to kill her!' he shouted as they took him into the elevator. 'She began screaming! I'm not a killer! Look at me! Do I look like a killer?' And then, as the elevator began dropping to the basement, he shouted, 'I'm a burglar!' as if proud of his profession, as if stating that he was something more than a common thief, a trained workman, a skilled artisan. 'I'm not a killer! I'm a burglar!' he screamed. 'I'm not a killer! I'm not a killer!' And his voice echoed down the elevator shaft as the car dropped to the basement and the waiting van.

They sat in the small room for several moments after he was gone.

'Hot in here,' Meyer said.

'Yeah.' Carella nodded.

'What's the matter?'

'Nothing.'

'Maybe he's right,' Meyer said. 'Maybe he's only a burglar.'

'He stopped being that the minute he stole a life, Meyer.'

'Josie Thompson stole a life, too.'

'No,' Carella said. He shook his head. 'She only borrowed one. There's a difference, Meyer.'

The room went silent.

'You feel like some coffee?' Meyer asked.

'Sure.'

They took the elevator down and then walked out into the brilliant August sunshine. The streets were teeming with life. They walked into the human swarm, but they were curiously silent.

At last Carella said, 'I guess I think she shouldn't be dead. I guess I think that someone who tried so hard to make a life shouldn't have had it taken away from her.'

Meyer put his hand on Carella's shoulder. 'Listen,' he said earnestly. 'It's a job. It's only a job.'

'Sure,' Carella said. 'It's only a job.'

'J'

1

It was the first of April, the day for fools.

It was also Saturday, and the day before Easter.

Death should not have come at all, but it had. And, having come, perhaps it was justified in its confusion. Today was the fool's day, the day for practical jokes. Tomorrow was Easter, the day of the bonnet and egg, the day for the spring march of finery and frills. Oh, yes, it was rumoured in some quarters of the city that Easter Sunday had something to do with a different sort of march at a place called Calvary, but it had been a long time since death was vetoed and rendered null and void, and people have short memories, especially where holidays are concerned.

Today, Death was very much in evidence, and plainly confused. Striving as it was to reconcile the trappings of two holidays – or perhaps three – it succeeded in producing only a blended distortion.

The young man who lay on his back in the alley was wearing black, as if in mourning. But over the black, in contradiction, was a fine silken shawl, fringed at both ends. He seemed dressed for spring, but this was the fool's day, and Death could not resist the temptation.

The black was punctuated with red and blue and white. The cobbled floor of the alley followed the same decorative scheme, red and blue and white, splashed about in gay spring abandon. Two overturned buckets of paint, one white, one blue, seemed to have ricocheted off the wall of the building and come to disorderly rest on the alley floor. The man's shoes were spattered with paint. His black garment was covered with paint. His hands were drenched in paint. Blue and white, white and blue, his black garment, his silken shawl, the floor of the alley, the brick wall of the building before which he lay – all were splashed with blue and white.

The third colour did not mix well with the others.

The third colour was red, a little too primary, a little too bright.

The third colour had not come from a paint can. The third colour still spilled freely from two dozen open wounds on the man's chest and stomach and neck and face and hands, staining the black, staining the silken shawl, spreading in a bright red pool on the alley floor, suffusing the paint with sunset, mingling with the paint but not mixing well, spreading until it touched the foot of the ladder lying crookedly along the wall, encircling the paintbrush lying at the wall's base. The bristles of the brush were still wet with white paint. The man's blood touched the bristles, and then trickled to the cement line where brick wall touched cobbled alley, flowing in an inching stream downwards towards the street.

Someone had signed the wall.

On the wall, someone had painted, in bright, white paint, the single letter J. Nothing more – only J.

The blood trickled down the alley to the city street.

Night was coming.

Detective Cotton Hawes was a tea drinker. He had picked up the habit from his minister father, the man who'd named him after Cotton Mather, the last of the red-hot Puritans. In the afternoons, the good Reverend Jeremiah Hawes had entertained members of his congregation, serving tea and cakes which his wife Matilda baked in the old, iron, kitchen oven. The boy, Cotton Hawes, had been allowed to join the tea-drinking congregation, thus developing a habit which had continued to this day.

At eight o'clock on the night of April first, while a young man lay in an alleyway with two dozen bleeding wounds shrieking in silence to the passersby on the street below, Hawes sat drinking tea. As a boy, he had downed the hot beverage in the book-lined study at the rear of the parish house, a mixture of Oolong and Pekoe which his mother brewed in the kitchen and served in English bone-china cups she had inherited from her grandmother. Tonight, he sat in the grubby, shopworn comfort of the 87th Precinct squadroom and drank, from a cardboard container, the tea Alf Miscolo had prepared in the clerical office. It was hot tea. That was about the most he could say for it.

The open, mesh-covered windows of the squadroom admitted a mild spring breeze from Grover Park across the way, a warm seductive breeze which made him wish he were outside on the street. It was criminal to be catching up on a night like this. It was also boring. Aside from one wife-beating squeal, which Steve Carella was out checking this very minute, the telephone had been ominously quiet. In the silence of the squadroom, Hawes had managed to type up three overdue DD reports, two chits for gasoline and a bulletin-board notice to the men of the squad reminding them that this was the first of the month and time for them to cough up fifty cents each for the maintenance of Alf Miscolo's improvised kitchen. He had also read a half-dozen FBI fliers, and listed in his little black memo book the licence-plate numbers of two more stolen vehicles.

Now he sat drinking insipid tea and wondering why it was so quiet. He supposed the lull had something to do with Easter. Maybe there was going to be an egg-rolling ceremony down South Twelfth Street tomorrow. Maybe all the criminals and potential criminals in the 87th were home dyeing. Eggs, that is. He smiled and took another sip of the tea. From the clerical office beyond the slatted rail divider which separated the squadroom from the corridor, he could hear the rattling of Miscolo's typewriter. Above that, and beyond it, coming from the iron-runged steps which led upstairs, he could hear the ring of footsteps. He turned towards the corridor just as Steve Carella entered it from the opposite end.

Carella walked easily and nonchalantly towards the railing, a big man who moved with fine-honed athletic precision. He shoved open the gate in the railing, walked to his desk, took off his jacket, pulled down his tie and unbuttoned the top button of his shirt.

'What happened?' Hawes asked.

'The same thing that always happens,' Carella said. He sighed heavily and rubbed his hand over his face. 'Is there any more coffee?' he asked.

'I'm drinking tea.'

'Hey, Miscolo!' Carella yelled. 'Any coffee in there?'

'I'll put on some more water!' Miscolo yelled back.

'So what happened?' Hawes asked.

'Oh, the same old jazz,' Carella said. 'It's a waste of time to even go out on these wife-beating squeals. I've never answered one yet that netted anything.'

'She wouldn't press charges,' Hawes said knowingly.

'Charges, hell. There wasn't even any beating, according to her. She's got blood running out of her nose, and a shiner the size of a half-dollar, and she's the one who screamed for the patrolman – but the minute I get there, everything's calm and peaceful.' Carella shook his head. ' "A beating, officer?" ' he mimicked in a high, shrill voice. ' "You must be mistaken, officer. Why, my husband is a good, kind, sweet man. We've been married for twenty years, and he never lifted a finger to me. You must be mistaken, sir." '

'Then who yelled for the cop?' Hawes asked.

'That's just what I said to her.'

'What'd she answer?'

'She said, "Oh, we were just having a friendly little family argument." The guy almost knocked three teeth out of her mouth, but that's just a friendly little family argument. So I asked her how she happened to have a bloody nose and a mouse under her eye and – catch this, Cotton – she said she got them ironing.'

'What?'

'Ironing.'

'Now, how the hell—'

'She said the ironing board collapsed and the iron jumped

up and hit her in the eye, and one of the ironing-board legs clipped her in the nose. By the time I left, she and her husband were ready to go on a second honeymoon. She was hugging him all over the place, and he was sneaking his hand under her dress, so I figured I'd come back here where it isn't so sexy.'

'Good idea,' Hawes said.

'Hey, Miscolo!' Carella shouted, 'Where's that coffee?'

'A watched pot never boils!' Miscolo shouted back cleverly.

'We've got George Bernard Shaw in the clerical office,' Carella said. 'Anything happen since I left?'

'Nothing. Not a peep.'

'The streets are quiet, too,' Carella said, suddenly thoughtful.

'Before the storm,' Hawes said.

'Mmmm.'

The squadroom was silent again. Beyond the meshed window, they could hear the myriad sounds of the city, the auto horns, the muffled cries, the belching of buses, a little girl singing as she walked past the station house.

'Well, I suppose I ought to type up some overdue reports,' Carella said.

He wheeled over a typing cart, took three Detective Division reports from his desk, inserted carbon between two of the sheets and began typing.

Hawes stared at the distant lights of Isola's buildings and sucked in a draught of mesh-filtered spring air.

He wondered why it was so quiet.

He wondered just exactly what all those people were doing out there.

Some of those people were playing April Fool's Day pranks. Some of them were getting ready for tomorrow, which was Easter Sunday. And some of them were celebrating a third and ancient holiday known as Passover. Now that's a coincidence which could cause one to speculate upon the similarity of dissimilar religions and the existence of a single, all-powerful God, and all that sort of mystic stuff, if one were inclined towards speculation. Speculator or not, it doesn't take a big detective to check a calendar, and the coincidence was there, take it or leave it. Buddhist, atheist, or Seventh Day Adventist, you had to admit there was something very democratic and wholesome about Easter and Passover coinciding the way they did, something which gave a festive air to the entire city. Jews and Gentiles alike, because of a chance mating of the Christian and Hebrew calendars, were celebrating important holidays at almost the same time. Passover had officially begun at sunset on Friday, March thirty-first, another coincidence, since Passover did not always fall on the Jewish Sabbath; but this year, it did. And tonight was April first, and the traditional second *seder* service, the annual re-enactment of the Jews' liberation from Egyptian bondage, was being observed in Jewish homes throughout the city.

Detective Meyer Meyer was a Jew.

Or at least, he thought he was a Jew. Sometimes he wasn't quite certain. Because if he was a Jew, he sometimes asked himself, how come he hadn't seen the inside of a synagogue in twenty years? And if he was a Jew, how come two of his favourite dishes were roast pork and broiled lobster, both of which were forbidden by the dietary laws of the religion? And if he was such a Jew, how come he allowed his son Alan – who was thirteen and who had been *barmitzvahed* only last month – to play Post Office with Alice McCarthy, who was as Irish as a four-leaf clover?

Sometimes, Meyer got confused.

Sitting at the head of the traditional table on this night of the second *seder*, he didn't know quite how he felt. He looked at his family, Sarah and the three children, and then he looked at the *seder* table, festively set with a floral centrepiece and lighted candles and the large platter upon which were placed the traditional objects – three matzos, a roasted shankbone, a roasted egg, bitter herbs, charoses, watercress – and he still didn't know exactly how he felt. He took a deep breath and began the prayer.

'And it was evening,' Meyer said, 'and it was morning,'

the sixth day. Thus the heaven and the earth were finished, and all the host of them. And on the seventh day, God had finished his work which He had made: and He rested on the seventh day from his work which he had done. And God blessed the seventh day, and hallowed it, because that in it He rested from all his work, which God had created in order to make it.'

There was a certain beauty to the words, and they lingered in his mind as he went through the ceremony, describing the various objects on the table and their symbolic meaning. When he elevated the dish containing the bone and the egg, everyone sitting around the table took hold of the dish, and Meyer said, 'This is the bread of affliction which our ancestors ate in the land of Egypt; let all those who are hungry, enter and eat thereof, and all who are in distress, come and celebrate the Passover.'

He spoke of his ancestors, but he wondered who he – their descendant – was.

'Wherefore is this night distinguished from all other nights?' he asked. 'Any other night, we may eat either leavened or unleavened bread, but on this night only unleavened bread; all other nights, we may eat any species of herbs, but on this night only bitter herbs ...'

The telephone rang. Meyer stopped speaking and looked at his wife. For a moment, both seemed reluctant to break the spell of the ceremony. And then Meyer gave a slight, barely discernible shrug. Perhaps, as he went to the telephone, he was recalling that he was a cop first, and a Jew only second.

'Hello?' he said.

'Meyer, this is Cotton Hawes.'

'What is it, Cotton?'

'Look, I know this is your holiday—'

'What's the trouble?'

'We've got a killing,' Hawes said.

Patiently, Meyer said, 'We've always got a killing.'

'This is different. A patrolman called in about five minutes ago. The guy was stabbed in the alley behind—'

'Cotton, I don't understand,' Meyer said. 'I switched the duty with Steve. Didn't he show up?'

'What is it, Meyer?' Sarah called from the dining room.

'It's all right, it's all right,' Meyer answered. 'Isn't Steve there?' he asked Hawes, annoyance in his voice.

'Sure, he's out on the squeal, but that's not the point.'

'What *is* the point?' Meyer asked. 'I was right in the middle of—'

'We need you on this one,' Hawes said. 'Look, I'm sorry as hell. But there are aspects to – Meyer, this guy they found in the alley—'

'Well, what about him?' Meyer asked.

'We think he's a rabbi,' Hawes said.

2

The sexton of the Isola Jewish Centre was named Yirmiyahu Cohen, and when he introduced himself, he used the Jewish word for sexton, *shamash*. He was a tall, thin man in his late fifties, wearing a sombre black suit and donning a skull-cap the moment he, Carella and Meyer re-entered the synagogue.

The three had stood in the alley behind the synagogue not a moment before, staring down at the body of the dead rabbi and the trail of mayhem surrounding him. Yirmiyahu had wept openly, his eyes closed, unable to look at the dead man who had been the Jewish community's spiritual leader. Carella and Meyer, who had both been cops for a good long time, did not weep.

There is plenty to weep at if you happen to be looking down at the victim of a homicidal stabbing. The rabbi's black robe and fringed prayer shawl were drenched with blood, but happily, they hid from view the multiple stab wounds in his chest and abdomen, wounds which would later be examined at the morgue for external description, number, location, dimension, form of perforation and direction and depth of penetration. Since twenty-five per cent of all fatal stab wounds are cases of cardiac penetration, and since there was a wild array of slashes and a sodden mass of coagulating blood near or around the rabbi's heart, the two detectives automatically assumed that a cardiac stab wound had been the cause of death, and were grateful for the fact that the rabbi was fully clothed. They had both visited the mortuary and seen naked bodies on naked slabs, no longer bleeding, all blood and all life drained away, but skin torn like the flimsiest cheesecloth, the soft interior of the body deprived of its protective flesh, turned outwards, exposed, the ripe wounds gaping and open, had stared at evisceration and wanted to vomit.

The rabbi now owned flesh, too, and at least a part of it had been exposed to his attacker's fury. Looking down at the dead man, neither Carella nor Meyer wanted to weep, but their eyes tightened a little and their throats went peculiarly dry because death by stabbing is a damn frightening thing. Whoever had handled the knife had done so in apparent frenzy. The only exposed areas of the rabbi's body were his hands, his neck, and his face – and these, more than the apparently fatal, hidden incisions beneath the black robe and the prayer shawl, shrieked bloody murder to the night. The rabbi's throat showed two superficial cuts which almost resembled suicidal hesitation cuts. A deeper horizontal slash at the front of his neck had exposed the trachea, carotids and jugular vein, but these did not appear to be severed – at least, not to the layman eyes of Carella and Meyer. There were cuts around the rabbi's eyes and a cut across the bridge of his nose.

But the wounds which caused both Carella and Meyer to turn away from the body were the slashes on the insides of the rabbi's hands. These, they knew, were the defence cuts.

These spoke louder than all the others, for they immediately reconstructed the image of a weaponless man struggling to protect himself against the swinging blade of an assassin, raising his hands in hopeless defence, the fingers cut and hanging, the palms slashed to ribbons. At the end of the alley, the patrolman who'd first arrived on the scene was identifying the body to the medical examiner as the one he'd found. Another patrolman was pushing curious bystanders behind the police barricade he'd set up. The laboratory boys and photographers had already begun their work.

Carella and Meyer were happy to be inside the synagogue again.

The room was silent and empty, a house of worship without any worshippers at the moment. They sat on folding chairs in the large, empty room. The eternal light burned over the ark in which the Torah, the five books of Moses, was kept. Forward of the ark, one on each side of it, were the lighted candelabra, the *menorah*, found by tradition in every Jewish house of worship.

Detective Steve Carella began the litany of another tradition. He took out his notebook, poised his pencil over a clean page, turned to Yirmiyahu, and began asking questions in a pattern that had become classic through repeated use.

'What was the rabbi's name?' he asked.

Yirmiyahu blew his nose and said, 'Solomon. Rabbi Solomon.'

'First name?'

'Yaakov.'

'That's Jacob,' Meyer said. 'Jacob Solomon.'

Carella nodded and wrote the name into his book.

'Are you Jewish?' Yirmiyahu asked Meyer.

Meyer paused for an instant, and then said, 'Yes.'

'Was he married or single?' Carella asked.

'Married,' Yirmiyahu said.

'Do you know his wife's name?'

'I'm not sure. I think it's Havah.'

'That's Eve,' Meyer translated.

'And would you know where the rabbi lived?'

'Yes. The house on the corner.'

'What's the address?'

'I don't know. It's the house with the yellow shutters.'

'How do you happen to be here right now, Mr Cohen?' Carella asked. 'Did someone call to inform you of the rabbi's death?'

'No. No, I often come past the synagogue. To check the light, you see.'

'What light is that, sir?' Carella asked.

'The eternal light. Over the ark. It's supposed to burn at all times. Many synagogues have a small electric bulb in the lamp. We're one of the few synagogues in the city who still use oil in it. And, as *shamash*, I felt it was my duty to make certain the light—'

'Is this an Orthodox congregation?' Meyer asked.

'No. It's Conservative,' Yirmiyahu said.

'There are three types of congregation now,' Meyer explained to Carella. 'Orthodox, Conservative and Reform. It gets a little complicated.'

'Yes,' Yirmiyahu said emphatically.

'So you were coming to the synagogue to check on the lamp,' Carella said. 'Is that right?'

'That's correct.'

'And what happened?'

'I saw a police car at the side of the synagogue. So I walked over and asked what the trouble was. And they told me.'

'I see. When was the last time you saw the rabbi alive, Mr Cohen?'

'At evening services.'

'Services start at sundown, Steve. The Jewish day—'

'Yes, I know,' Carella said. 'What time did services end, Mr Cohen?'

'At about seven-thirty.'

'And the rabbi was here? Is that right?'

'Well, he stepped outside when services were over.'

'And you stayed inside. Was there any special reason?'

'Yes. I was collecting the prayer shawls and the *yarmelkas*, and I was putting—'

'*Yarmelkas* are skullcaps,' Meyer said. 'Those little black—'

'Yes, I know,' Carella said. 'Go ahead, Mr Cohen.'

'I was putting the *rimonim* back on to the handles of the scroll.'

'Putting the what, sir?' Carella asked.

'Listen to the big Talmudic scholar,' Meyer said, grinning. 'Doesn't even know what *rimonim* are. They're these decorative silver covers, Steve, shaped like pomegranates. Symbolizing fruitfulness, I guess.'

Carella returned the grin. 'Thank you,' he said.

'A man has been killed,' Yirmiyahu said softly.

The detectives were silent for a moment. The banter between them had been of the faintest sort, mild in comparison to some of the grisly humour that homicide detectives passed back and forth over a dead body. Carella and Meyer were accustomed to working together in an easy, friendly manner, and they were accustomed to dealing with the facts of sudden death, but they realized at once that they had offended the dead rabbi's sexton.

'I'm sorry, Mr Cohen,' he said. 'We meant no offence, you understand.'

The old man nodded stoically, a man who had inherited a legacy of years and years of persecution, a man who automatically concluded that all Gentiles looked upon a Jew's life as a cheap commodity. There was unutterable sadness on his long, thin face, as if he alone were bearing the oppressive weight of the centuries on his narrow shoulders.

The synagogue seemed suddenly smaller. Looking at the old man's face and the sadness there, Meyer wanted to touch it gently and say, 'It's all right, *tsadik*, it's all right,' the Hebrew word leaping into his mind – *tsadik*, a man possessed of saintly virtues, a person of noble character and simple living.

The silence persisted. Yirmiyahu Cohen began weeping

again, and the detectives sat in embarrassment on the folding chairs and waited.

At last Carella said, 'Were you still here when the rabbi came inside again?'

'I left while he was gone,' Yirmiyahu said. 'I wanted to return home. This is the *Pesach*, the Passover. My family was waiting for me to conduct the *seder*.'

'I see.' Carella paused. He glanced at Meyer.

'Did you hear any noise in the alley, Mr Cohen?' Meyer asked. 'When the rabbi was out there?'

'Nothing.'

Meyer sighed and took a package of cigarettes from his jacket pocket. He was about to light one when Yirmiyahu said, 'Didn't you say you were Jewish?'

'Huh?' Meyer said. He struck the match.

'You are going to *smoke* on the second day of *Pesach*?' Yirmiyahu asked.

'Oh. Oh, well ...' The cigarette felt suddenly large in Meyer's hand, the fingers clumsy. He shook out the match. 'You – uh – you have any other questions, Steve?' he asked.

'No,' Carella said.

'Then I guess you can go, Mr Cohen,' Meyer said. 'Thank you very much.'

'*Shalom*,' Yirmiyahu said, and shuffled dejectedly out of the room.

'You're not supposed to smoke, you see,' Meyer explained to Carella, 'on the first two days of Passover, and the last two, a good Jew doesn't smoke, or ride, or work, or handle money or—'

'I thought this was a Conservative synagogue,' Carella said. 'That sounds like Orthodox practice to me.'

'Well, he's an old man,' Meyer said. 'I guess the customs die hard.'

'The way the rabbi did,' Carella said grimly.

3

They stood outside in the alley where chalk marks outlined the position of the dead body. The rabbi had been carted away, but his blood still stained the cobblestones, and the rampant paint had been carefully side-stepped by the laboratory boys searching for footprints and fingerprints, searching for anything which would provide a lead to the killer.

'J,' the wall read.

'You know, Steve, I feel funny on this case,' Meyer told Carella.

'I do, too.'

Meyer raised his eyebrows, somewhat surprised. 'How come?'

'I don't know. I guess because he was a man of God.' Carella shrugged. 'There's something unworldly and naïve and – pure, I guess – about rabbis and priests and ministers and I guess I feel they shouldn't be touched by all the dirty things in life.' He paused. 'Somebody's got to stay untouched, Meyer.'

'Maybe so,' Meyer paused. 'I feel funny because I'm a Jew, Steve.' His voice was very soft. He seemed to be confessing something he would not have admitted to another living soul.

'I can understand that,' Carella said gently.

'Are you policemen?'

The voice startled them. It came suddenly from the other end of the alley, and they both whirled instantly to face it.

Instinctively, Meyer's right hand reached for the service revolver holstered in his right rear pocket.

'Are you policemen?' the voice asked again. It was a woman's voice, thick with a Yiddish accent. The street lamp was behind the owner of the voice. Meyer and Carella saw only a frail figure clothed in black, pale white hands clutched to the breast of the black coat, pinpoints of light burning where the woman's eyes should have been.

'We're policemen,' Meyer answered. His hand hovered near the butt of his pistol. Beside him, he could feel Carella tensed for a draw.

'I know who killed the *rov*,' the woman said.

'What?' Carella asked.

'She says she knows who killed the rabbi,' Meyer whispered in soft astonishment.

His hand dropped to his side. They began walking towards the street end of the alley. The woman stood there motionless, the light behind her, her face in shadow, the pale hands still, her eyes burning.

'Who killed him?' Carella said.

'I know the *rotsayach*,' the woman answered. 'I know the murderer.'

'Who?' Carella said again.

'Him!' the woman shouted, and she pointed to the painted white J on the synagogue wall. 'The *sonei Yisroel*! Him!'

'The anti-Semite,' Meyer translated. 'She says the anti-Semite did it.'

They had come abreast of the woman now. The three stood at the end of the alley with the street lamp casting long shadows on the cobbles. They could see her face. Black hair and brown eyes, the classic Jewish face of a woman in her fifties, the beauty stained by age and something else, a fine-drawn tension hidden in her eyes and on her mouth.

'What anti-Semite?' Carella asked. He realized he was whispering. There was something about the woman's face and the blackness of her coat and the paleness of her hands which made whispering a necessity.

'On the next block,' she said. Her voice was a voice of judgement and doom. 'The one they call Finch.'

'You saw him kill the rabbi?' Carella asked. 'You saw him do it?'

'No.' She paused. 'But I know in my heart that he's the one . . .'

'What's your name, ma'am?' Meyer asked.

'Hannah Kaufman,' she said. 'I know it was him. He said he would do it, and now he has started.'

'He said he would do what?' Meyer asked the old woman patiently.

'He said he would kill all the Jews.'

'You heard him say this?'

'*Everyone* has heard him.'

'His name is Finch?' Meyer asked her. 'You're sure?'

'Finch,' the woman said. 'On the next block. Over the candy store.'

'What do you think?' he asked Carella.

Carella nodded. 'Let's try him.'

4

If America is a melting pot, the 87th Precinct is a crucible. Start at the River Harb, the northernmost boundary of the precinct territory, and the first thing you hit is exclusive Smoke Rise, where the walled-in residents sit in white-Protestant respectability in houses set a hundred feet back from private roads, admiring the greatest view the city has to offer. Come out of Smoke Rise and hit fancy Silvermine Road where the aristocracy of apartment buildings have begun to submit to the assault of time and the encroachment of the surrounding slums. Forty-thousand-dollar-a-year executives still live in these apartment buildings, but people write on the walls here, too: limericks, prurient slogans, which industrious doormen try valiantly to erase.

There is nothing so eternal as Anglo-Saxon etched in graphite.

Silvermine Park is south of the Road, and no one ventures there at night. During the day, the park is thronged with governesses idly chatting about the last time they saw Sweden, gently rocking shellacked blue baby buggies. But after sunset, not even lovers will enter the park. The Stem, further south, explodes the moment the sun leaves the sky. Gaudy and incandescent, it mixes Chinese restaurants with Jewish delicatessens, pizza joints with Greek cabarets offering belly dancers. Threadbare as a beggar's sleeve, Ainsley Avenue crosses the centre of the precinct, trying to maintain a dignity long gone, crowding the sidewalks with austere but dirty apartment buildings, furnished rooms, garages and a sprinkling of sawdust saloons. Culver Avenue turns completely Irish with the speed of a leprechaun. The faces, the bars, even the buildings seem displaced, seem to have been stolen and transported from the centre of Dublin; but no lace curtains hang in the windows. Poverty turns a naked face to the streets here, setting the pattern for the rest of the precinct territory. Poverty rakes the back of the Culver Avenue Irish, claws its way on to the white and tan and brown and black faces of the Puerto Ricans lining Mason Avenue, flops on to the beds of the whores on *La Vía de Putas*, and then pushes its way into the real crucible, the city side streets where different minority groups live cheek by jowl, as close as lovers, hating each other. It is here that Puerto Rican and Jew, Italian and Negro, Irishman and Cuban are forced by dire economic need to live in a ghetto which, by its very composition, loses definition and becomes a meaningless tangle of unrelated bloodlines.

Rabbi Solomon's synagogue was on the same street as a Catholic church. A Baptist store-front mission was on the avenue leading to the next block. The candy store over which the man named Finch lived was owned by a Puerto Rican whose son had been a cop – a man named Hernandez.

Carella and Meyer paused in the lobby of the building and studied the name plates in the mailboxes. There were eight boxes in the row. Two had name plates. Three had broken locks. The man named Finch lived in apartment thirty-three on the third floor.

The lock on the vestibule door was broken. From behind the stairwell, where the garbage cans were stacked before being put out for collection in the morning, the stink of that evening's dinner remains assailed the nostrils and left the detectives mute until they had gained the first-floor landing.

On the way up to the third floor, Carella said, 'This seems too easy, Meyer. It's over before it begins.'

On the third-floor landing, both men drew their service revolvers. They found apartment thirty-three and bracketed the door.

'Mr Finch?' Meyer called.

'Who is it?' a voice answered.

'Police. Open up.'

The apartment and the hallway went still.

'Finch?' Meyer said.

There was no answer. Carella backed off against the opposite wall. Meyer nodded. Bracing himself against the wall, Carella raised his right foot, the leg bent at the knee, then released it like a triggered spring. The flat of his sole collided with the door just below the lock. The door burst inwards, and Meyer followed it into the apartment, his gun in his fist.

Finch was a man in his late twenties, with a square crew-cut head and bright green eyes. He was closing the closet door as Meyer burst into the room. He was wearing only trousers and an undershirt, his feet bare. He needed a shave, and the bristles on his chin and face emphasized a white scar that ran from just under his right cheek to the curve of his jaw. He turned from the closet with the air of a man who has satisfactorily completed a mysterious mission.

'Hold it right there,' Meyer said.

There's a joke they tell about an old woman on a train who repeatedly asks the man sitting beside her if he's Jewish. The man, trying to read his newspaper, keeps answering, 'No, I'm not Jewish.' The old lady keeps pestering him, tugging at his sleeve, asking the same question over and over again. Finally the man puts down his newspaper and says, 'All right, all right, damn it! I'm Jewish.'

And the old lady smiles at him sweetly and says, 'You know something? You don't look it.'

The joke, of course, relies on a prejudice which assumes that you can tell a man's religion by looking at his face.

There was nothing about Meyer Meyer's looks or speech which would indicate that he was Jewish. His face was round and clean-shaven, he was thirty-seven years old and completely bald, and he possessed the bluest eyes this side of Denmark. He was almost six feet tall and perhaps a trifle overweight, and the only conversation he'd had with Finch were the few words he'd spoken through the closed door, and the four words he'd spoken since he entered the apartment, all of which were delivered in big-city English without any noticeable trace of accent.

But when Meyer Meyer said, 'Hold it right there,' a smile came on to Finch's face, and he answered, 'I wasn't going anyplace, Jewboy.'

Well, maybe the sight of the rabbi lying in his own blood had been too much for Meyer. Maybe the words '*sonei Yisroel*' had recalled the days of his childhood when, one of the few Orthodox Jews in a Gentile neighbourhood, and bearing the double-barrelled name his father had foisted upon him, he was forced to defend himself against every hoodlum who crossed his path, invariably against overwhelming odds. He was normally a very patient man. He had borne his father's practical joke with amazing good will, even though he sometimes grinned mirthlessly through bleeding lips. But tonight, this second night of Passover, after having looked down at the bleeding rabbi, after having heard the tortured sobs of the sexton, after having seen the patiently suffering face of the woman in black, the words hurled at him from the other end of the apartment had a startling effect.

Meyer said nothing. He simply walked to where Finch was standing near the closet, and lifted the .38 high above his head. He flipped the gun up as his arm descended, so that the heavy butt was in striking position as it whipped towards Finch's jaw.

Finch brought up his hands, but not to shield his face in defence. His hands were huge, with big knuckles, the imprimatur of the habitual street fighter. He opened the fingers and caught Meyer's descending arm at the wrist, stopping the gun three inches from his face.

He wasn't dealing with a kid; he was dealing with a cop. He obviously intended to shake that gun out of Meyer's fist and then beat him senseless on the floor of the apartment. But Meyer brought up his right knee and smashed it into Finch's groin, and then, his wrist still pinioned, he bunched his left fist and drove it hard and straight into Finch's gut. That did it. The fingers loosened and Finch backed away a step just as Meyer brought the pistol back across his own body and then unleashed it in a backhand swipe. The butt cracked against Finch's jaw and sent him sprawling against the closet wall.

Miraculously, the jaw did not break. Finch collided with the closet, grabbed the door behind him with both hands opened wide and flat against the wood, and then shook his head. He blinked his eyes and shook his head again. By what seemed to be sheer will power, he managed to stand erect without falling on his face.

Meyer stood watching him, saying nothing, breathing hard. Carella, who had come into the room, stood at the far end, ready to shoot Finch if he so much as raised a pinky.

'Your name Finch?' Meyer asked.

'I don't talk to Jews,' Finch answered.

'Then try *me*,' Carella said. 'What's your name?'

'Go to hell, you and your Jewboy friend both.'

Meyer did not raise his voice. He simply took a step closer to Finch, and very softly said, 'Mister, in two minutes, you're gonna be a cripple because you resisted arrest.'

He didn't have to say anything else, because his eyes told the full story, and Finch was a fast reader.

'Okay,' Finch said, nodding. 'That's my name.'

'What's in the closet, Finch?' Carella asked.

'My clothes.'

'Get away from the door.'

'What for?'

Neither of the cops answered. Finch studied them for ten seconds, and quickly moved away from the door. Meyer opened it. The closet was stacked high with piles of tied and bundled pamphlets. The cord on one bundle was untied, the pamphlets spilling on to the closet floor. Apparently, this bundle was the one Finch had thrown into the closet when he'd heard the knock on the door. Meyer stooped and picked up one of the pamphlets. It was badly and cheaply printed, but the intent was unmistakable. The title of the pamphlet was 'The Bloodsucker Jew'.

'Where'd you get this?' Meyer asked.

'I belong to a book club,' Finch answered.

'There are a few laws against this sort of thing,' Carella said.

'Yeah?' Finch answered. 'Name me one.'

'Happy to. Section 1340 of the Penal Law – libel defined.'

'Maybe you ought to read Section 1342,' Finch said, *'The publication is justified when the matter charged as libellous is true, and was published with good motives and for justifiable ends.'*

'Then let's try Section 514,' Carella said. *'"A person who denies or aids or incites another to deny any person because of race, creed, colour or national origin ..."'*

'I'm not trying to incite anyone,' Finch said, grinning.

'Nor am I a lawyer,' Carella said. 'But we can also try Section 700, which defines discrimination, and Section 1430, which makes it a felony to perform an act of malicious injury to a place of religious worship.'

'Huh?' Finch said.

'Yeah,' Carella answered.

'What the hell are you talking about?'

'I'm talking about the little paint job you did on the synagogue wall.'

'What paint job? What synagogue?'

'Where were you at eight o'clock tonight, Finch?'

'Out.'

'Where?'

'I don't remember.'

'You better *start* remembering.'

'Why? Is there a section of the Penal Law against loss of memory?'

'No,' Carella said. 'But there's one against homicide.'

95

5

The team stood around him in the squadroom.

The team consisted of Detectives Steve Carella, Meyer Meyer, Cotton Hawes, and Bert Kling. Two detectives from Homicide South had put in a brief appearance to legitimize the action, and then went home to sleep, knowing full well that the investigation of a homicide is always left to the precinct discovering the stiff. The team stood around Finch in a loose semicircle. This wasn't a movie sound stage, so there wasn't a bright light shining in Finch's eyes, nor did any of the cops lay a finger on him. These days, there were too many smart-assed lawyers around who were ready and able to leap upon irregular interrogation methods when and if a case finally came to trial. The detectives simply stood around Finch in a loose, relaxed semicircle, and their only weapons were a thorough familiarity with the interrogation process and with each other, and the mathematical superiority of four minds pitted against one.

'What time did you leave the apartment?' Hawes asked.

'Around seven.'

'And what time did you return?' Kling asked.

'Nine, nine-thirty. Something like that.'

'Where'd you go?' Carella asked.

'I had to see somebody.'

'A rabbi?' Meyer asked.

'No.'

'Who?'

'I don't want to get anybody in trouble.'

'You're in plenty of trouble yourself,' Hawes said. 'Where'd you go?'

'No place.'

'Okay, suit yourself,' Carella said. 'You've been shooting your mouth off about killing Jews, haven't you?'

'I never said anything like that.'

'Where'd you get these pamphlets?'

96

'I found them.'

'You agree with what they say?'

'Yes.'

'You know where the synagogue in this neighbourhood is?'

'Yes.'

'Were you anywhere near it tonight between seven and nine?'

'No.'

'Then where were you?'

'No place.'

'Anybody see you there?' Kling asked.

'See me where?'

'The no place you went to.'

'Nobody saw me.'

'You went no place,' Hawes said, 'and nobody saw you. Is that right?'

'That's right.'

'The invisible man,' Kling said.

'That's right.'

'When you get around to killing all these Jews,' Carella said, 'how do you plan to do it?'

'I don't plan to kill anybody,' he said defensively.

'Who you gonna start with?'

'Nobody.'

'Ben-Gurion?'

'Nobody.'

'Or maybe you've already started.'

'I didn't kill anybody, and I'm not gonna kill anybody. I want to call a lawyer.'

'A Jewish lawyer?'

'I wouldn't have—'

'What wouldn't you have?'

'Nothing.'

'You like Jews?'

'No.'

'You hate them?'

'No.'

'Then you like them.'

'No. I didn't say—'

'You either like them or you hate them. Which?'

'That's none of your goddamn business!'

'But you agree with the crap in those hate pamphlets, don't you?'

'They're not hate pamphlets.'

'What do you call them?'

'Expressions of opinion.'

'Whose opinion?'

'*Everybody's* opinion!'

'Yours included?'

'Yes, mine included!'

'Do you know Rabbi Solomon?'

'No.'

'What do you think of rabbis in general?'

'I never think of rabbis.'

'But you think of Jews a lot, don't you?'

'There's no crime about think—'

'If you think of Jews you must think of rabbis. Isn't that right?'

'Why should I waste my time—'

'The rabbi is the spiritual leader of the Jewish people, isn't he?'

'I don't know anything about rabbis.'

'But you must know that.'

'What if I do?'

'Well, if you said you were going to kill the Jews—'

'I never said—'

'—then a good place to start would be with—'

'I never said anything like that!'

'We've got a witness who heard you! A good place to start would be with a rabbi, isn't that so?'

'Go shove your rabbi—'

'Where were you between seven and nine tonight?'

'No place.'

'You were behind that synagogue, weren't you?'

'No.'

'You were painting a J on the wall, weren't you?'
'No! No, I wasn't!'
'You were stabbing a rabbi!'
'You were killing a Jew!'
'I wasn't any place near that—'
'Book him, Cotton. Suspicion of murder.'
'Suspicion of— I'm telling you I wasn't—'
'Either shut up or start talking, you bastard,' Carella said.
Finch shut up.

6

The girl came to see Meyer Meyer on Easter Sunday.

She had reddish-brown hair and brown eyes, and she wore a dress of bright persimmon with a sprig of flowers pinned to the left breast. She stood at the railing and none of the detectives in the squadroom even noticed the flowers; they were too busy speculating on the depth and texture of the girl's rich curves.

The girl didn't say a word. She didn't have to. The effect was almost comic, akin to the cocktail-party scene where the voluptuous blonde takes out a cigarette and four hundred men are stampeded in the rush to light it. The first man to reach the slatted rail divider was Cotton Hawes, since he was single and unattached. The second man was Hal Willis, who was also single and a good red-blooded American boy. Meyer Meyer, an old married poop, contented himself with ogling the girl from behind his desk. The word *shtik* crossed Meyer's mind, but he rapidly pushed the thought aside.

'Can I help you, miss?' Hawes and Willis asked simultaneously.

'I'd like to see Detective Meyer,' the girl said.

'Meyer?' Hawes asked, as if his manhood had been maligned.

'Meyer?' Willis repeated.

'Is he the man handling the murder of the rabbi?'

'Well we're *all* sort of working on it,' Hawes said modestly.

'I'm Artie Finch's girlfriend,' the girl said. 'I want to talk to Detective Meyer.'

Meyer rose from his desk with the air of a man who has been singled out from the stag line by the belle of the ball. Using his best radio announcer's voice, and his best company manners, he said, 'Yes, miss, I'm Detective Meyer.'

He held open the gate in the railing, all but executed a bow, and led the girl to his desk. Hawes and Kling watched as the girl sat and crossed her legs. Meyer moved a pad into place with all the aplomb of a General Motors executive.

'I'm sorry, miss,' he said. 'What was your name?'

'Eleanor,' she said. 'Eleanor Fay.'

'F-A-Y-E?' Meyer asked, writing.

'F-A-Y.'

'And you're Arthur Finch's fiancée? Is that right?'

'I'm his girlfriend,' Eleanor corrected.

'You're not engaged?'

'Not officially, no.' She smiled demurely, modestly and sweetly. Across the room, Cotton Hawes rolled his eyes towards the ceiling.

'What did you want to see me about, Miss Fay?' Meyer asked.

'I wanted to see you about Arthur. He's innocent. He didn't kill that man.'

'I see. What do you know about it, Miss Fay?'

'Well, I read in the paper that the rabbi was killed sometime between seven-thirty and nine. I think that's right, isn't it?'

'Approximately, yes.'

'Well, Arthur couldn't have done it. I know where he was during that time.'

'And where was he?' Meyer asked.

He figured he knew just what the girl would say. He had heard the same words from an assortment of molls, mistresses, fiancées, girlfriends and just plain acquaintances of men accused of everything from disorderly conduct to first-degree murder. The girl would protest that Finch was with her during that time. After a bit of tooth-pulling, she would admit that – well – they were alone together. After a little more coaxing, the girl would reluctantly state, the reluctance adding credulity to her story, that – well – they were alone in intimate circumstances together. The alibi having been firmly established, she would then wait patiently for her man's deliverance.

'And where was he?' Meyer asked, and waited patiently.

'From seven to eight,' Eleanor said, 'he was with a man named Bret Loomis in a restaurant called The Gate, on Culver and South Third.'

'What?' Meyer was surprised.

'Yes. From there, Arthur went to see his sister in Riverhead. I can give you the address if you like. He got there at about eight-thirty and stayed a half-hour or so. Then he went straight home.'

'What time did he get home?'

'Ten o'clock.'

'He told us nine, nine-thirty.'

'He was mistaken. I know he got home at ten because he called me the minute he was in the house. It was ten o'clock.'

'I see. And he told you he'd just got home?'

'Yes.' Eleanor Fay nodded and uncrossed her legs. Willis, at the water cooler, did not miss the sudden revealing glimpse of nylon and thigh.

'Did he also tell you he'd spent all that time with Loomis first and then with his sister?'

'Yes, he did.'

'Then why didn't he tell *us*?' Meyer asked.

'I don't know why. Arthur is a person who respects family and friends. I suppose he didn't want to involve them with the police.'

'That's very considerate of him,' Meyer said drily, 'especially since he's being held on suspicion of murder. What's his sister's name?'

'Irene Granavan. Mrs Carl Granavan.'

'And her address?'

'Nineteen-eleven Morris Road. In Riverhead.'

'Know where I can find this Bret Loomis?'

'He lives in a rooming house on Culver Avenue. The address is 3918. It's near Fourth.'

'You came pretty well prepared, didn't you, Miss Fay?' Meyer asked.

'If you don't come prepared,' Eleanor answered, 'why come at all?'

7

Bret Loomis was thirty-one years old, five feet six inches tall, bearded. When he admitted the detectives to the apartment, he was wearing a bulky black sweater and tight-fitting dungarees. Standing next to Cotton Hawes, he looked like a little boy who had tried on a false beard in an attempt to get a laugh out of his father.

'Sorry to bother you, Mr Loomis,' Meyer said. 'We know this is Easter, and—'

'Oh, yeah?' Loomis said. He seemed surprised. 'Hey, that's right, ain't it? It's Easter. I'll be damned. Maybe I oughta go out and buy myself a pot of flowers.'

'You didn't know it was Easter?' Hawes asked.

'Like, man, who ever reads the newspapers? Gloom, gloom! I'm fed up to here with it. Let's have a beer, celebrate Easter. Okay?'

'Well, thanks,' Meyer said, 'but—'

'Come on, so it ain't allowed. Who's gonna know besides you, me and the bedpost? Three beers coming up.'

Meyer looked at Hawes and shrugged. Hawes shrugged back. Together, they watched Loomis as he went to the refrigerator in one corner of the room and took out three bottles of beer.

'Sit down,' he said. 'You'll have to drink from the bottle because I'm a little short of glasses. Sit down, sit down.'

The detectives glanced around the room, puzzled.

'Oh,' Loomis said, 'you'd better sit on the floor. I'm a little short of chairs.'.

The three men squatted around a low table which had obviously been made from a tree stump. Loomis put the bottles on the table top, lifted his own bottle, said 'Cheers,' and took a long drag at it.

'What do you do for a living, Mr Loomis?' Meyer asked.

'I live,' Loomis said.

'What?'

'I *live* for a living. That's what I do.'

'I meant, how do you support yourself?'

'I get payment from my ex-wife.'

'*You* get payments?' Hawes asked.

'Yeah. She was so delighted to get rid of me that she made a settlement. A hundred bucks a week. That's pretty good, isn't it?'

'That's very good,' Meyer said.

'You think so?' Loomis seemed thoughtful. 'I think I coulda boosted it to *two* hundred if I held out a little longer. The bitch was running around with another guy, you see, and was all hot to marry him He's got plenty of loot. I bet I coulda boosted it to two hundred.'

'How long do these payments continue?' Hawes asked, fascinated.

'Until I get married again – which I will never ever do as long as I live. Drink your beer. It's good beer.' He took a drag at his bottle and said, 'What'd you want to see me about?'

'Do you know a man named Arthur Finch?'

'Sure. He in trouble?'

'Yes.'

'What'd he do?'

'Well, let's skip that for the moment, Mr Loomis,' Hawes said. 'We'd like you to tell us—'

'Where'd you get that white streak in your hair?' Loomis asked suddenly.

'Huh?' Hawes touched his left temple unconsciously. 'Oh, I got knifed once. It grew back this way.'

'All you need is a blue streak on the other temple. Then you'll look like the American flag,' Loomis said, and laughed.

'Yeah,' Hawes said. 'Mr Loomis, can you tell us where you were last night between seven and eight o'clock?'

'Oh, boy,' Loomis said, 'this is like "Dragnet", ain't it? "Where were you on the night of December twenty-first? All we want are the facts."'

'Just like "Dragnet",' Meyer said drily. 'Where were you, Mr Loomis?'

'Last night? Seven o'clock?' He thought for a moment. 'Oh, sure.'

'Where?'

'Olga's pad.'

'Who?'

'Olga Trenovich. She's like a sculptress. She does these crazy little statues in wax. Like she drips the wax all over everything. You dig?'

'And you were with her last night?'

'Yeah. She had like a little session up at her pad. A couple of coloured guys on sax and drums and two other kids on trumpet and piano.'

'You got there at seven, Mr Loomis?'

'No. I got there at six-thirty.'

'And what time did you leave?'

'Gosssshhhhh, who remembers?' Loomis said. 'It was the wee, small hours.'

'After midnight, you mean?' Hawes asked.

'Oh, sure. Two, three in the morning,' Loomis said.

'You got there at six-thirty and left at two or three in the morning? Is that right?'

'Yeah.'

'Was Arthur Finch with you?'

'Hell, no.'

'Did you see him at all last night?'

'Nope. Haven't seen him since – let me see – last month sometime.'

'You were *not* with Arthur Finch in a restaurant called The Gate?'

'When? Last night, you mean?'

'Yes.'

'Nope. I just told you. I haven't seen Artie in almost two weeks.' A sudden spark flashed in Loomis' eyes and he looked at Hawes and Meyer guiltily.

'Oh-oh,' he said. 'What'd I just do? Did I screw up Artie's alibi?'

'You screwed it up fine, Mr Loomis,' Hawes said.

8

Irene Granavan, Finch's sister, was a twenty-one-year-old girl who had already borne three children and was working on her fourth, in her fifth month of pregnancy. She admitted the detectives to her apartment in a Riverhead housing development, and then immediately sat down.

'You have to forgive me,' she said. 'My back aches. The doctor thinks maybe it'll be twins. That's all I need is twins.' She pressed the palms of her hands into the small of her back, sighed heavily, and said, 'I'm always having a baby. I got married when I was seventeen, and I've been pregnant ever since. All my kids think I'm a fat woman. They've never seen me that I wasn't pregnant.' She sighed again. 'You got any children?' she asked Meyer.

'Three,' he answered.

'I sometimes wish ...' She stopped and pulled a curious face, a face which denied dreams.

'What do you wish, Mrs Granavan?' Hawes asked.

'That I could go to Bermuda. Alone.' She paused. 'Have you ever been to Bermuda?'

'No.'

'I hear it's very nice there,' Irene Granavan said wistfully, and the apartment went still.

'Mrs Granavan,' Meyer said, 'we'd like to ask you a few questions about your brother.'

'What's he done now?'

'Has he done things before?' Hawes said.

'Well, you know ...' She shrugged.

'What?' Meyer asked.

'Well, the fuss down at City Hall. And the picketing of that movie. You know.'

'We don't know, Mrs Granavan.'

'Well, I hate to say this about my own brother, but I think he's a little nuts on the subject. You know.'

'What subject?'

'Well, the movie, for example. It's about Israel, and him and his friends picketed it and all, and handed out pamphlets about Jews, and ... You remember, don't you? The crowd threw stones at him and all. There were a lot of concentration-camp survivors in the crowd, you know.' She paused. 'I think he must be a little nuts to do something like that, don't you think?'

'You said something about City Hall, Mrs Granavan. What did your brother—'

'Well, it was when the mayor invited this Jewish assemblyman – I forget his name – to make a speech with him on the steps of City Hall. My brother went down and – well, the same business. You know.'

'You mentioned your brother's friends. What friends?'

'The nuts he hangs out with.'

'Would you know their names?' Meyer wanted to know.

'I know only one of them. He was here once with my

106

brother. He's got pimples all over his face. I remember him because I was pregnant with Sean at the time, and he asked if he could put his hands on my stomach to feel the baby kicking. I told him he certainly could not. That shut *him* up, all right.'

'What was his name, Mrs Granavan?'

'Fred. That's short for Frederick. Frederick Schultz.'

'He's German?' Meyer asked.

'Yes.'

Meyer nodded briefly.

'Mrs Granavan,' Hawes said, 'was your brother here last night?'

'Why? Did he say he was?'

'Was he?'

'No.'

'Not at all?'

'No. He wasn't here last night. I was home alone last night. My husband bowls on Saturdays.' She paused. 'I sit at home and hug my fat belly, and he bowls. You know what I wish sometimes?'

'What?' Meyer asked.

And, as if she had not said it once before, Irene Granavan said, 'I wish I could go to Bermuda sometime. Alone.'

'The thing is,' the house painter said to Carella. 'I'd like my ladder back.'

'I can understand that,' Carella said.

'The brushes they can keep, although some of them are very expensive brushes. But the ladder I absolutely need. I'm losing a day's work already because of those guys down at your lab.'

'Well, you see—'

'I go back to the synagogue this morning, and my ladder and my brushes and even my paints are all gone. And what a mess somebody made of that alley! So this old guy who's sexton of the place, he tells me the priest was killed Saturday night, and the cops took all the stuff away with them. I wanted to know what cops, and he said he didn't know. So I called Headquarters this morning, and I got a runaround from six different cops who finally put me through to some guy named Grossman at the lab.'

'Yes, Lieutenant Grossman,' Carella said.

'That's right. And he tells me I can't have my goddamn ladder back until they finish their tests on it. Now what the hell do they expect to find on my ladder, would you mind telling me?'

'I don't know, Mr Cabot. Fingerprints, perhaps.'

'Yeah, *my* fingerprints! Am I gonna get involved in murder *besides* losing a day's work?'

'I don't think so,' Carella said, smiling.

'I shouldn't have taken that job, anyway,' Cabot said. 'I shouldn't have even bothered with it.'

'Who hired you for the job, Mr Cabot?'

'The priest did.'

'The rabbi, you mean?' Carella asked.

'Yeah, the priest, the rabbi, whatever the hell you call him.' Cabot shrugged.

'And what were you supposed to do, Mr Cabot?'

'I was supposed to paint. What do you think I was supposed to do?'

'Paint what?'

'The trim. Around the windows and the roof.'

'White and blue?'

'White around the windows, and blue for the roof trim.'

'The colours of Israel,' Carella said.

'Yeah,' the painter agreed. Then he said, 'What?'

'Nothing. Why did you say you shouldn't have taken the job, Mr Cabot?'

'Well, because of all the arguing first. He wanted it done for Peaceable, he said, and Peaceable fell on the first. But I couldn't—'

'Peaceable? You mean Passover?'

'Yeah, Peaceable, Passover, whatever the hell you call it.' He shrugged again.

'You were about to say?'

'I was about to say we had a little argument about it. I

was working on another job, and I couldn't get to his job until Friday, the thirty-first. I figured I'd work late into the night, you know, but the priest told me I couldn't work after sundown. So I said why can't I work after sundown, so he said the Sabbath began at sundown, not to mention the first day of Peace— Passover, and that work wasn't allowed on the first two days of Passover, nor on the Sabbath neither, for that matter. Because the Lord rested on the Sabbath, you see. The seventh day.'

'Yes, I see.'

'Sure. So I said, "Father, I'm not of the Jewish faith," is what I said, "and I can work any day of the week I like." Besides, I got a big job to start on Monday, and I figured I could knock off the church all day Friday and Friday night or, if worse came to worse, Saturday, for which I usually get time and a half. So we compromised.'

'How did you compromise?'

'Well, this priest was of what you call the Conservative crowd, not the Reformers, which are very advanced, but still these Conservatives don't follow all the old rules of the religion is what I gather. So he said I could work during the day Friday, and then I could come back and work Saturday, provided I knocked off at sundown. Don't ask me what kind of crazy compromise it was. I think he had in mind that he holds mass at sundown and it would be a mortal sin if I was outside painting while everybody was inside praying, and on a very special high holy day, at that.'

'I see. So you painted until sundown Friday?'

'Right.'

'And then you came back Saturday morning?'

'Right. But what it was, the windows needed a lot of putty, and the sills needed scraping and sanding, so by sundown Saturday, I still wasn't finished with the job. I had a talk with the priest, who said he was about to go inside and pray, and could I come back after services to finish off the job? I told him I had a better idea. I would come back Monday morning and knock off the little bit that had to be done before I went on to this very big job I got in Majesta – it's painting a whole factory; that's a big job. So I left everything right where it was in back of the church. I figured, who'd steal anything from right behind a church. Am I right?'

'Right,' Carella said.

'Yeah. Well, you know who'd steal them from right behind a church?'

'Who?'

'The cops!' Cabot shouted. 'That's who! Now how the hell do I get my ladder back, would you please tell me? I got a call from the factory today. They said if I don't start work tomorrow, at the latest, I can forget all about the job. And me without a ladder!'

'Maybe we've got a ladder downstairs you can borrow,' Carella said.

'Mister, I need a tall painter's ladder. This is a very high factory. Can you call this Captain Grossman and ask him to please let me have my ladder back? I got mouths to feed.'

'I'll talk to him, Mr Cabot,' Carella said. 'Leave me your number, will you?'

'I tried to borrow my brother-in-law's ladder – he's a paper hanger – but he's papering this movie star's apartment, downtown on Jefferson. So just try to get *his* ladder. Just try.'

'Well, I'll call Grossman,' Carella said.

'The other day, what she done, this movie actress, she marched into the living room wearing only this towel, you see? She wanted to know what—'

'I'll call Grossman,' Carella said.

As it turned out, he didn't have to call Grossman, because a lab report arrived late that afternoon, together with Cabot's ladder and the rest of his working equipment, including his brushes, his putty knife, several cans of linseed oil and turpentine, a pair of paint-stained gloves and two dropcloths. At about the same time the report arrived, Grossman called from downtown, saving Carella a dime.

'Did you get my report?' Grossman asked.

'I was just reading it.'

'What do you make of it?'

'I don't know,' Carella said.

'Want my guess?'

'Sure I'm always interested in what the layman thinks,' Carella answered him

'Layman, I'll give you a hit on the head!' Grossman answered laughing. 'You notice the rabbi's prints were on those paint-can lids, and also on the ladder?'

'Yes, I did.'

'The ones on the lids were thumb prints, so I imagine the rabbi put those lids back on to the paint cans or, if they were already on the cans, pushed down on them to make sure they were secure.'

'Why would he want to do that?'

'Maybe he was moving the stuff. There's a tool shed behind the synagogue. Had you noticed that?'

'No, I hadn't.'

'Tch-tch, big detective. Yeah, there's one there, all right, about fifty yards behind the building. So I figure the painter rushed off, leaving his junk all over the back yard, and the rabbi was moving it to the tool shed when he was surprised by the killer.'

'Well, the painter did leave his stuff there, that's true. He expected to come back Monday morning.'

'Today, yeah,' Grossman said. 'But maybe the rabbi figured he didn't want his back yard looking like a pigsty, especially since this is Passover. So he took it into his head to move the stuff over to the tool shed. This is just speculation, you understand.'

'No kidding?' Carella said. 'I thought it was sound, scientific deduction.'

'Go to hell. Those *are* thumb prints on the lids, so it's logical to conclude he pressed down on them. And the prints on the ladder seem to indicate he was carrying it.'

'This report said you didn't find any prints but the rabbi's,' Carella said. 'Isn't that just a little unusual?'

'You didn't read it right,' Grossman said. 'We found a portion of a print on one of the paintbrushes. And we also—'

'Oh yeah,' Carella said, 'here it is. This doesn't say much, Sam.'

'What do you want me to do? It seems to be a tented-arch pattern, like the rabbi's, but there's too little to tell. The print could have been left on that brush by someone else.'

'Like the painter?'

'No. We've pretty much decided the painter used gloves while he worked. Otherwise, we'd have found a flock of similar prints on all the tools.'

'Then who left that print on the brush? The killer?'

'Maybe.'

'But the portion isn't enough to get anything positive on?'

'Sorry, Steve.'

'So your guess on what happened is that the rabbi went outside after services to clean up the mess. The killer surprised him, knifed him, made a mess of the alley, and then painted that J on the wall. Is that it?'

'I guess so, though—'

'What?'

'Well, there was a lot of blood leading right over to that wall, Steve. As if the rabbi had crawled there after he'd been stabbed.'

'Probably trying to get to the back door of the synagogue.'

'Maybe,' Grossman said. 'One thing I can tell you. Whoever killed him must have been pretty much of a mess when he got home. No doubt about that.'

'Why do you say that?'

'That spattered paint all over the alley,' Grossman said. 'It's my guess that the rabbi threw those paint cans at his attacker.'

'You're a pretty good guesser, Sam,' Carella told him, grinning.

'Thanks,' Grossman said.

'Tell me something.'

'Yeah?'

'You ever solve any murders?'

'Go to hell,' Grossman said, and he hung up.

9

Alone with his wife that night in the living room of their apartment, Meyer tried to keep his attention *off* a television series about cops and *on* the various documents he had collected from Rabbi Solomon's study in the synagogue. The cops on television were shooting up a storm, blank bullets flying all over the place and killing hoodlums by the score. It almost made a working man like Meyer Meyer wish for an exciting life of romantic adventure.

The romantic adventure of *his* life, Sarah Lipkin Meyer, sat in an easy chair opposite the television screen, her legs crossed, absorbed in the fictional derring-do of the policemen.

'Ooooh, *get* him!' Sarah screamed at one point, and Meyer turned to look at her curiously, and then went back to the rabbi's books.

The rabbi kept a ledger of expenses, all of which had to do with the synagogue and his duties there. The ledger did not make interesting reading, and told Meyer nothing he wanted to know. The rabbi also kept a calendar of synagogue events and Meyer glanced through them reminiscently, remembering his own youth and the busy Jewish life centring around the synagogue in the neighbourhood adjacent to his own. *March twelfth,* the calendar read, *regular Sunday breakfast of the Men's Club. Speaker, Harry Pine, director of Commission on International Affairs of American Jewish Congress. Topic: The Eichmann Case.*

Meyer's eye ran down the list of events itemized in Rabbi Solomon's book:

12 March, 7.15 p.m.
Youth Group meeting.

18 March, 9.30 a.m.
Bar Mitzvah services for Nathan Rothman. Kiddush after services. Open invitation to Centre membership.

22 March, 8.45 p.m.
Clinton Samuels, Assistant Professor of Philosophy in

113

Education, Brandeis University, will lead discussion in 'The Matter of Identity for the Jews in Modern America'.

26 March
Eternal Light Radio. 'The Search' by Virginia Mazer, biographical script on Lillian Wald, founder of Henry Street Settlement in New York.

Meyer looked up from the calendar. 'Sarah?' he said.

'Shhh, shhh, just a minute,' Sarah answered. She was nibbling furiously at her thumb, her eyes glued to the silent television screen. An ear-shattering volley of shots suddenly erupted, all but smashing the picture tube. The theme music came up, and Sarah let out a deep sigh and turned to her husband.

Meyer looked at her curiously, as if seeing her for the first time, remembering the Sarah Lipkin of long, long ago and wondering if the Sarah Meyer of today was very much different from that initial exciting image. 'Nobody's lips kin like Sarah's lips kin,' the fraternity boys had chanted, and Meyer had memorized the chant, and investigated the possibilities, learning for the first time in his life that every cliché bears a kernel of folklore. He looked at her mouth now, pursed in puzzlement as she studied his face. Her eyes were blue, and her hair was brown, and she had a damn good figure and splendid legs, and he nodded in agreement with his youthful judgement.

'Sarah, do you feel any identity as a Jew in modern America?' he asked.

'What?' Sarah said.

'I said—'

'Oh, boy,' Sarah said. 'What brought *that* on?'

'The rabbi, I guess.' Meyer scratched his bald pate. 'I guess I haven't felt so much like a Jew since – since I was confirmed, I guess. It's a funny thing.'

'Don't let it trouble you,' Sarah said gently. 'You *are* a Jew.'

'Am I?' he asked, and he looked straight into her eyes.

She returned the gaze. 'You have to answer that one for yourself,' she said.

'I know I – well, I get mad as hell thinking about this guy

114

Finch. Which isn't good, you know. After all, maybe he's innocent.'

'Do you think so?'

'No. I think he did it. But is it *me* who thinks that, Meyer Meyer, Detective Second Grade? Or is it Meyer Meyer who got beat up by the *goyim* when he was a kid, and Meyer Meyer who heard his grandfather tell stories about pogroms, or who listened to the radio and heard what Hitler was doing in Germany, or who nearly strangled a German colonel with his bare hands just outside—'

'You can't separate the two, darling,' Sarah said.

'Maybe you can't. I'm only trying to say I never much felt like a Jew until this case came along. Now, all of a sudden ...' He shrugged.

'Shall I get your prayer shawl?' Sarah said, smiling.

'Wise guy,' Meyer said. He closed the rabbi's calendar, and opened the next book on the desk. The book was a personal diary. He unlocked it, and began leafing through it.

Friday, 6 January
Shabbat, Parshat Shemot. I lighted the candles at 4.24. Evening services were at 6.15. It has been a hundred years since the Civil War. We discussed the Jewish Community of the South, then and now.

18 January
It seems odd to me that I should have to familiarize the membership about the proper blessings over the Sabbath candles. Have we come so far towards forgetfulness?

Baruch ata adonai elohenu melech haolam asher kidshanu b'mitzvotav vitzivanu l'hadlick ner shel shabbat.

Blessed are Thou O Lord our God, King of the universe who hast sanctified us by Thy laws and commanded us to kindle the Sabbath Light.

Perhaps he is right. Perhaps the Jews are doomed.

20 January
I had hoped that the Maccabean festival would make us realize the hardships borne by the Jews 2,000 years ago in comparison to our good and easy lives today in a democracy. Today, we have the freedom to worship as we desire, but this should

impose upon us the responsibility of enjoying that freedom. And yet Hanukkah has come and gone, and it seems to me The Feast of Lights taught us nothing, gave us nothing more than a joyous holiday to celebrate.

The Jews will die, he says.

2 February

I believe I am beginning to fear him. He shouted threats at me today, said that I, of all the Jews, would lead the way to destruction. I was tempted to call the police, but I understand he has done this before. There are those in the membership who have suffered his harangues and who seemed to feel he is harmless. But he rants with the fervour of a fanatic, and his eyes frighten me.

12 February

A member called today to ask me something about the dietary laws. I was forced to call the local butcher because I did not know the prescribed length of the *hallaf*, the slaughtering knife. Even the butcher, in jest, said to me that a real rabbi would know these things. I *am* a real rabbi. I believe in the Lord, my God, I teach His will and His law to His people. What need a rabbi know about *shehitah*, the art of slaughtering animals? Is it important to know that the slaughtering knife must be twice the width of the throat of the slaughtered animal, and no more than fourteen finger breadths in length? The butcher told me that the knife must be sharp and smooth, with no perceptible notches. It is examined by passing finger and fingernail over both edges of the blade before and after slaughtering. If a notch is found, the animal is then unfit. Now I know. But is it necessary to know this? Is it not enough to love God, and to teach His ways?

His anger continues to frighten me.

14 February

I found a knife in the ark today, at the rear of the cabinet behind the Torah.

8 March

We had no further use of the Bibles we replaced, and since they were old and tattered, but nonetheless ritual articles containing the name of God, we buried them in the back yard, near the tool shed.

I must see about contacting a painter to do the outside of the synagogue. Someone suggested a Mr Frank Cabot who lives in the neighbourhood. I will call him tomorrow, perhaps. Passover will be coming soon, and I would like the temple to look nice.

The mystery is solved. It is kept for trimming the wick in the oil lamp over the ark.

The telephone rang. Meyer, absorbed in the diary, didn't even hear it. Sarah went to the phone and lifted it from the cradle.

'Hello?' she said. 'Oh, hello, Steve. How are you?' She laughed and said, 'No, I was watching television. That's right.' She laughed again. 'Yes, just a minute, I'll get him.' She put the phone down and walked to where Meyer was working. 'It's Steve,' she said. 'He wants to speak to you.'

'Huh?'

'The phone. Steve.'

'Oh,' Meyer nodded. 'Thanks.' He walked over to the phone and lifted the receiver. 'Hello, Steve,' he said.

'Hi. Can you get down here right away?'

'Why? What's the matter?'

'Finch,' Carella said. 'He's broken jail.'

10

Finch had been kept in the detention cells of the precinct house all day Sunday where, it being Easter, he had been served turkey for his midday meal. On Monday morning, he'd been transported by van to Headquarters downtown on High Street where, as a felony offender, he participated in that quaint police custom known simply as 'the line-up'. He had been mugged and printed afterwards in the basement of the building, and then led across the street to the Criminal Courts Building where he had been arraigned for first-degree murder and, over his lawyer's protest, ordered to be held without bail until trial. The police van had then transported him crosstown to the house of detention on Canopy Avenue where he'd remained all day Monday, until after the evening meal. At that time, those offenders who had committed, or who were alleged to have committed, the most serious crimes, were once more shackled and put into the van, which carried them uptown and south to the edge of the River Dix for transportation by ferry to the prison on Walker Island.

He'd made his break, Carella reported, while he was being moved from the van to the ferry. According to what the harbour police said, Finch was still handcuffed and wearing prison garb. The break had taken place at about ten p.m. It was assumed that it had been witnessed by several dozen hospital attendants waiting for the ferry which would take them to Dix Sanitarium, a city-owned-and-operated hospital for drug addicts, situated in the middle of the river about a mile and a half from the prison. It was also assumed that the break had been witnessed by a dozen or more water rats who leaped among the dock pilings and who, because of their size, were sometimes mistaken for pussy cats by neighbourhood kids who played near the river's edge. Considering the fact that Finch was dressed in drab grey uniform and hand-cuffs – a dazzling display of sartorial elegance, to be sure, but not likely to be seen on any other male walking the city streets – it was amazing that he hadn't yet been picked up. They had, of course, checked his apartment first, finding nothing there but the four walls and the furniture. One of the unmarried detectives on the squad, probably hoping for an invitation to go along, suggested that they look up Eleanor Fay, Finch's girl. Wasn't it likely he'd head for her pad? Carella and Meyer agreed that it was entirely likely, clipped their holsters on, neglected to offer the invitation to their colleague, and went out into the night.

It was a nice night, and Eleanor Fay lived in a nice neigh-bourhood of old brownstones wedged in between new, all-glass apartment houses with garages below the sidewalk.

April had danced across the city and left her subtle warmth in the air. The two men drove in one of the squad's sedans, the windows rolled down. They did not say much to each other, April had robbed them of speech. The police radio droned its calls endlessly; radio motor patrolmen all over the city acknowledged violence and mayhem.

'There it is,' Meyer said. 'Just up ahead.'

'Now try to find a parking spot,' Carella complained.

They circled the block twice before finding an opening in front of a drugstore on the avenue. They got out of the car, left it unlocked, and walked briskly in the balmy night. The brownstone was in the middle of the block. They climbed the twelve steps to the vestibule, and studied the name plates alongside the buzzers. Eleanor Fay was in apartment 2B. Without hesitation, Carella pressed the buzzer for apartment 5A. Meyer took the doorknob in his hand and waited. When the answering click came, he twisted the knob, and silently they headed for the steps to the second floor.

Kicking in a door is an essentially rude practice. Neither Carella nor Meyer were particularly lacking in good manners, but they were looking for a man accused of murder, and a man who had successfully broken jail. It was not unnatural to assume this was a desperate man, and so they didn't even discuss whether or not they would kick in the door. They aligned themselves in the corridor outside apartment 2B. The wall opposite the door was too far away to serve as a springboard. Meyer, the heavier of the two men, backed away from the door, then hit it with his shoulder. He hit it hard and close to the lock. He wasn't attempting to shatter the door itself, an all but impossible feat. All he wanted to do was spring the lock. All the weight of his body concentrated in the padded spot of arm and shoulder which collided with the door just above the lock. The lock itself remained locked, but the screws holding it to the jamb could not resist the force of Meyer's fleshy battering ram. The wood around the screws splintered, the threads lost their friction grip, the door shot inwards and Meyer followed it into the room. Carella, like a quarterback carrying the ball behind powerful interference, followed Meyer.

119

It's rare that a cop encounters raw sex in his daily routine. The naked bodies he sees are generally cold and covered with caked blood. Even vice-squad cops find the act of love sordid rather than enticing. Eleanor Fay was lying full length on the living-room couch with a man. The television set in front of the couch was going, but nobody was watching either the news or the weather.

When the two men with drawn guns piled into the room behind the imploding door, Eleanor Fay sat bolt upright on the couch, her eyes wide in surprise. She was naked to the waist. She was wearing tight-fitting black tapered slacks and black high-heeled pumps. Her hair was disarranged and her lipstick had been kissed from her mouth, and she tried to cover her exposed breasts with her hands the moment the cops entered, realized the task was impossible, and grabbed the nearest article of clothing, which happened to be the man's suit jacket. She held it up in front of her like the classic, surprised heroine in a pirate movie. The man beside her sat up with equal suddenness, turned towards the cops, then turned back to Eleanor, puzzled, as if seeking an explanation from her.

The man was not Arthur Finch.

He was a man in his late twenties. He had a lot of pimples on his face, and a lot of lipstick stains. His white shirt was open to the waist. He wore no undershirt.

'Hello, Miss Fay,' Meyer said.

'I didn't hear you knock,' Eleanor answered. She seemed to recover instantly from her initial surprise and embarrassment. With total disdain for the two detectives, she threw the jacket aside, rose and walked like a burlesque queen to a hard-backed chair over which her missing clothing was draped. She lifted a brassière, shrugged into it, clasped it, all as if she were alone in the room. Then she pulled a black, long-sleeved sweater over her head, shook out her hair, lighted a cigarette, and said. 'Is breaking and entering only a crime for criminals?'

'We're sorry, Miss,' Carella said. 'We're looking for your boyfriend.'

'Me?' the man on the couch asked. 'What'd *I* do?'

A glance of puzzlement passed between Meyer and Carella. Something like understanding, faint and none too clear, touched Carella's face.

'Who are you?' he said.

'You don't have to tell them anything,' Eleanor cautioned. 'They're not allowed to break in like this. Private citizens have rights, too.'

'That's right, Miss Fay,' Meyer said. 'Why'd you lie to us?'

'I didn't lie to anybody.'

'You gave us false information about Finch's whereabouts on—'

'I wasn't aware I was under oath at the time.'

'You weren't. But you were damn well maliciously impeding the progress of an investigation.'

'The hell with you *and* your investigation. You horny bastards bust in here like—'

'We're sorry we spoiled your party,' Carella said. 'Why'd you lie about Finch?'

'I thought I was helping you,' Eleanor said. 'Now get the hell out of here.'

'We're staying a while, Miss Fay,' Meyer said, 'so get off your high horse. How'd you figure you were helping us? By sending us on a wild-goose chase confirming alibis you knew were false?'

'I didn't know anything. I told you just what Arthur told me.'

'That's a lie.'

'Why don't you get out?' Eleanor said. 'Or are you hoping I'll take off my sweater again?'

'What you've got, we've already seen, lady,' Carella said. He turned to the man. 'What's your name?'

'Don't tell him,' Eleanor said.

'Here or uptown, take your choice,' Carella said. 'Arthur Finch has broken jail, and we're trying to find him. If you want to be accessories to—'

'Broken jail?' Eleanor went a trifle pale. She glanced at the man on the couch, and their eyes met.

'Wh-when did this happen?' the man asked.

'About ten o'clock tonight.'

The man was silent for several moments. 'That's not so good,' he said at last.

'How about telling us who you are,' Carella suggested.

'Frederick Schultz,' the man said.

'That makes it all very cosy, doesn't it?' Meyer said.

'Get your mind out of the gutter,' Eleanor said. 'I'm not Finch's girl, and I never was.'

'Then why'd you say you were?'

'I didn't want Freddie to get involved in this thing.'

'How could he possibly get involved?'

Eleanor shrugged.

'What is it? Was Finch with Freddie on Saturday night?'

Eleanor nodded reluctantly.

'From what time to what time?'

'From seven to ten,' Freddie said.

'Then he couldn't have killed the rabbi.'

'Who said he did?' Freddie answered.

'Why didn't you tell us this?'

'Because ...' Eleanor started, and then stopped dead.

'Because they had something to hide,' Carella said. 'Why'd he come to see you, Freddie?'

Freddie did not answer.

'Hold it,' Meyer said. 'This is the other Jew-hater, Steve. The one Finch's sister told me about. Isn't that right, Freddie?'

Freddie did not answer.

'Why'd he come to see you, Freddie? To pick up those pamphlets we found in his closet?'

'You the guy who prints that crap, Freddie?'

'What's the matter, Freddie? Weren't you sure how much of a crime was involved?'

'Did you figure he'd tell us where he got the stuff, Freddie?'

'You're a real good pal, aren't you, Freddie? You'd send your friend to the chair rather than—'

'I don't owe him anything!' Freddie said.

'Maybe you owe him a lot. He was facing a murder rap, but he never once mentioned your name. You went to all that trouble for nothing, Miss Fay.'

'It was no trouble,' Eleanor said thinly.

'No,' Meyer said. 'You marched into the precinct with a tight dress and a cockamamie bunch of alibis that you knew we'd check. You figured once we found those to be phony, we wouldn't believe anything else Finch said. Even if he told us where he *really* was, we wouldn't believe it. That's right, isn't it?'

'You finished?' Eleanor asked.

'No, but I think you are,' Meyer answered.

'You had no right to bust in here. There's no law against making love.'

'Sister,' Carella said, '*you* were making hate.'

11

Arthur Finch wasn't making anything when they found him.

They found him at ten minutes past two, on the morning of April fourth. They found him in his apartment because a patrolman had been sent there to pick up the pamphlets in his closet. They found him lying in front of the kitchen table. He was still handcuffed. A file and rasp were on the table top, and there were metal filings covering the enamel and a spot on the linoleum floor, but Finch had made only a small dent in the manacles. The filings on the floor were floating in a red, sticky substance.

Finch's throat was open from ear to ear.

The patrolman, expecting to make a routine pickup, found the body and had the presence of mind to call his patrol-car partner before he panicked. His partner went down to the car and radioed the homicide to Headquarters, who informed Homicide South and the detectives of the 87th Squad.

The patrolmen were busy that night. At three a.m., a citizen called in to report what he thought was a leak in a water main on South Fifth. The radio dispatcher at Headquarters sent a car to investigate, and the patrolman found that nothing was wrong with the water main, but something was interfering with the city's fine sewage system.

The men were not members of the Department of Sanitation, but they nonetheless climbed down a manhole into the stink and garbage, and located a man's black suit caught on an orange crate and blocking a pipe, causing the water to back up into the street. The man's suit was spattered with white and blue paint. The patrolmen were ready to throw it into the nearest garbage can when one of them noticed it was also spattered with something that could have been dried blood. Being conscientious law-enforcement officers, they combed the garbage out of their hair and delivered the garment to their precinct house – which happened to be the 87th.

Meyer and Carella were delighted to receive the suit.

It didn't tell them a goddamned thing about who owned it, but it nonetheless indicated to them that whoever had killed the rabbi was now busily engaged in covering his tracks and this, in turn, indicated a high state of anxiety. Somebody had heard the news broadcast announcing Finch's escape. Somebody had been worried about Finch establishing an alibi for himself that would doubtlessly clear him.

With twisted reasoning somebody figured the best way to cover one homicide was to commit another. And somebody had hastily decided to get rid of the garments he'd worn while disposing of the rabbi.

The detectives weren't psychologists, but two mistakes had been committed in the same early morning, and they figured their prey was getting slightly desperate.

'It has to be another of Finch's crowd,' Carella said. 'Whoever killed Solomon painted a J on the wall. If he'd had time, he probably would have drawn a swastika as well.'

'But why would he do that?' Meyer asked. 'He'd automatically be telling us that an anti-Semite killed the rabbi.'

'So? How many anti-Semites do you suppose there are in this city?'

'How many?' Meyer asked.

'I wouldn't want to count them,' Carella said. 'Whoever killed Yaakov Solomon was bold enough to—'

'Jacob,' Meyer corrected.

'Yaakov, Jacob, what's the difference? The killer was bold enough to presume there were plenty of people who felt *exactly* the way he did. He painted that J on the wall and dared us to find *which* Jew-hater had done the job.' Carella paused. 'Does this bother you very much, Meyer?'

'Sure, it bothers me.'

'I mean, my saying—'

'Don't be a boob, Steve.'

'Okay. I think we ought to look up this woman again. What was her name? Hannah something. Maybe she knows—'

'I don't think that'll help us. Maybe we ought to talk to the rabbi's wife. There's indication in his diary that he knew the killer, that he'd had threats. Maybe she knows who was baiting him.'

'It's four o'clock in the morning,' Carella said. 'I don't think it's a good idea right now.'

'We'll go after breakfast.'

'It won't hurt to talk to Yirmiyahu again, either. If the rabbi was threatened, maybe—'

'Jeremiah,' Meyer corrected.

'What?'

'Jeremiah. Yirmiyahu is Hebrew for Jeremiah.'

'Oh. Well, anyway, him. It's possible the rabbi took him into his confidence, mentioned this—'

'Jeremiah,' Meyer said again.

'What?'

'No.' Meyer shook his head. 'That's impossible. He's a holy man. And if there's anything a really good Jew despises, it's—'

'What are you talking about?' Carella said.

'—it's killing. Judaism teaches that you don't murder, unless

125

in self-defence.' His brow suddenly furrowed into a frown. 'Still, remember when I was about to light that cigarette? He asked me if I was Jewish – remember? He was shocked that I would smoke on the second day of Passover.'

'Meyer, I'm a little sleepy. Who are you talking about?' Carella wanted to know.

'Yirmiyahu. Jeremiah. Steve, you don't think—'

'I'm just not following you, Meyer.'

'You don't think ... you don't think the rabbi painted that wall *himself*, do you?'

'Why would ... what do you mean?'

'To tell us who'd stabbed him? To tell us who the killer was?'

'How would—'

'Jeremiah,' Meyer said.

Carella looked at Meyer silently for a full thirty seconds. Then he nodded and said, 'J.'

12

He was burying something in the back yard behind the synagogue when they found him. They had gone to his home first and awakened his wife. She was an old Jewish woman, her head shaved in keeping with the Orthodox tradition. She covered her head with a shawl, and she sat in the kitchen of her ground-floor apartment and tried to remember what had happened on the second night of Passover. Yes, her husband had gone to the synagogue for evening services. Yes, he had come home directly after services.

'Did you see him when he came in?' Meyer asked.

'I was in the kitchen,' Mrs Cohen answered. 'I was preparing the *seder*. I heard the door open, and he went in the bedroom.'

'Did you see what he was wearing?'

'No.'

'What was he wearing during the *seder*?'

'I don't remember.'

'Had he changed his clothes, Mrs Cohen? Would you remember that?'

'I think so, yes. He had on a black suit when he went to temple. I think he wore a different suit after.' The old woman looked bewildered. She didn't know why they were asking these questions. Nonetheless, she answered them.

'Did you smell anything strange in the house, Mrs Cohen?'

'Smell?'

'Yes. Did you smell paint?'

'Paint? No. I smelled nothing strange.'

They found him in the yard behind the synagogue.

He was an old man with sorrow in his eyes and in the stoop of his posture. He had a shovel in his hands, and he was patting the earth with the blade. He nodded, as if he knew why they were there. They faced each other across the small mound of freshly turned earth at Yirmiyahu's feet.

Carella did not say a solitary word during the questioning and arrest. He stood next to Meyer Meyer, and he felt only an odd sort of pain.

'What did you bury, Mr Cohen?' Meyer asked. He spoke very softly. It was five o'clock in the morning, and night was fleeing the sky. There was a slight chill on the air. The wind seemed to penetrate to the sexton's marrow. He seemed on the verge of shivering. 'What did you bury, Mr Cohen? Tell me.'

'A ritual object,' the sexton answered.

'*What*, Mr Cohen?'

'I have no further use for it. It is a ritual object. I am sure it had to be buried. I must ask the *rov*. I must ask him what the Talmud says.' Yirmiyahu fell silent. He looked at the mound of earth at his feet. 'The *rov* is dead, isn't he?' he said, almost to himself. 'He is dead.' He looked sadly into Meyer's eyes.

'Yes,' Meyer answered.

'*Baruch dayyan haemet,*' Yirmiyahu said. 'You are Jewish?'

'Yes,' Meyer answered.

'Blessed be God the true judge,' Yirmiyahu translated, as if he had not heard Meyer.

'What did you bury, Mr Cohen?'

'The knife,' Yirmiyahu said. 'The knife I used to trim the wick. It *is* a ritual object, don't you think? It should be buried, don't you think?' He paused. 'You see ...' His shoulders began to shake. He began weeping suddenly. 'I killed,' he said. The sobs started somewhere deep within the man, started wherever his roots were, started in the soul of the man, in the knowledge that he had committed the unspeakable crime – thou shalt not kill, thou shalt not kill. 'I killed,' he said again, but this time there were only tears, no sobs.

'Did you kill Arthur Finch?' Meyer asked.

The sexton nodded.

'Did you kill Rabbi Solomon?'

'He ... you see ... he was working. It was the second day of Passover, and he was working. I was inside when I heard the noise. I went to look and ... he was carrying paints, paint cans in one hand, and ... a ladder in the other. He was *working.* I ... took the knife from the ark, the knife I used to trim the wick. I had told him before this. I had told him he was not a *real* Jew, that his new ... his new ways would be the end of the Jewish people. And this, *this*! To work on the second day of Passover!'

'What happened, Mr Cohen?' Meyer asked gently.

'I – the knife was in my hand. I went at him with the knife. He – he tried to stop me. He threw paint at me. I – I–' The sexton's right hand came up as if clasped around a knife. The hand trembled as it unconsciously re-enacted the events of that night. 'I cut him. I cut him ... I killed him.'

Yirmiyahu stood in the alley with the sun intimidating the peaks of the buildings now. He stood with his head bent, staring down at the mound of earth which covered the buried knife. His face was thin and gaunt, a face tormented by the centuries. The tears still spilled from his eyes and coursed down his cheeks. His shoulders shook with the sobs that came from somewhere deep in his guts. Carella turned away because it seemed to him in that moment that he was watching the disintegration of a man, and he did not want to see it.

Meyer put his arm around the sexton's shoulder.

'Come, *tsadik*,' he said. 'Come. You must come with me now.'

The old man said nothing. His hands hung loosely at his sides.

They began walking slowly out of the alley. As they passed the painted J on the synagogue wall, the sexton said. *'Olov hashalom.'*

'What did he say?' Carella asked.

'He said, "Peace be upon him." '

'Amen,' Carella said.

They walked silently out of the alley together.

Storm

1

The girl with Cotton Hawes had cold feet.

He didn't know what to do about her feet because he'd already tried everything he could think of, and they were still cold. He had to admit that driving in subzero temperatures with a storm some fifteen minutes behind him wasn't exactly conducive to warm pedal extremities. But he had turned the car heater up full, supplied the girl with a blanket, taken off his overcoat and wrapped that around her – and she still had cold feet.

The girl's name was Blanche Colby, a very nice euphonic name which she had adopted the moment she entered show business. That had been a long time ago. Blanche's real name was Bertha Cooley, but a press agent those many years back told her that Bertha Cooley sounded like a mentholated Pullman, and not a dancer. Blanche Colby had class, he told her, and if there was one thing Bertha Cooley wanted, it was class. She had taken the new name and gone into the chorus of a hit musical twenty-two years ago, when she was only fifteen. She was now thirty-seven, but all those years of prancing the boards had left her with a youthful body, lithe and long-legged. She was still, with a slight assist from Clairol, a soft honey-blonde. Her green eyes were intelligent and alert. Her feet, unfortunately, *ahhhh*, her feet.

'How are they now?' he asked her.

'Freezing,' she said.

'We're almost there,' Hawes told her. 'You'll like this place.

One of the guys on the squad – Hal Willis – comes up here almost every weekend he's off. He says the skiing is great.'

'I know a dancer who broke her leg in Switzerland,' Blanche said.

'Skiing?'

'Sure, skiing.'

'You've never skied before?'

'Never.'

'Well . . .' Hawes shrugged. 'Well, I don't think you'll break any legs.'

'That's reassuring,' Blanche said. She glanced through the window on her side of the car. 'I think that storm is catching up to us.'

'Just a few flurries.'

'I wonder how serious it'll be. I have a rehearsal Monday night.'

'Four to six inches, they said. That's not very much.'

'Will the roads be open?'

'Sure. Don't worry.'

'I know a dancer who got snowed in for six days in Vermont,' Blanche said. 'It wouldn't have been so bad, but she was with a Method actor.'

'Well, I'm a cop,' Hawes said.

'Yeah,' Blanche answered noncommittally.

They were silent for several moments. The light snow flurries drifted across the road, turning it into a dreamlike, white, flowing stream. The headlights illuminated the shifting macadam. Sitting behind the wheel, Hawes had the peculiar feeling that the road was melting. He was glad to see the sign for Rawson Mountain Inn. He stopped the car, picking out the sign from the tangle of other signs announcing accommodations in the area. He set the car in motion again, turning left over an old wooden bridge, the timbers creaking as the convertible passed over them. A new sign, blatant red and white, shouted the features of the area – a sixteen-hundred-foot mountain, two chair lifts, a T-Bar, a rope tow, and, definitely not needed with a storm on the way, a snow-making machine.

The inn lay nestled in the foothills at the base of the mountain. The trees around the inn were bare, standing in gaunt silhouette against the snow-threatening sky. Snow-nuzzled lights beckoned warmly. He helped Blanche out of the car, put on his overcoat, and walked with her over old packed snow to the entrance. They stamped their feet in the doorway and entered the huge room. A fire was going at one end of the room. Someone was playing the piano. A handful of tired weekday skiers were sprawled around the fireplace, wearing very fashionable after-ski boots and sweaters, drinking from bottles on to which they'd hand-lettered their names. Blanche went directly to the fire, found a place on one of the couches, and stretched her long legs to the blaze. Hawes found the desk, tapped a bell on it, and waited. No one appeared. He tapped the bell again. A skier passing the desk said, 'He's in the office. Over there on your left.'

Hawes nodded, found the door marked OFFICE, and knocked on it. A voice inside called, 'Yes, come in,' and Hawes twisted the knob and entered.

The office was larger than he'd expected, a good fifteen feet separating the entrance door from the desk at the opposite end of the room. A man in his late twenties sat behind the desk. He had dark hair and dark brows pulled low over deep brown eyes. He was wearing a white shirt open at the throat, a bold reindeer-imprinted sweater over it. He was also wearing a plaster cast on his right leg. The leg was stretched out stiffly in front of him, the foot resting on a low ottoman. A pair of crutches leaned against the desk, within easy reach of his hands. Hawes was suddenly glad he'd left Blanche by the fire.

'You're not a new skier, I hope,' the man said.

'No, I'm not.'

'Good. Some of them get scared by the cast and crutches.'

'Was it a skiing accident?' Hawes asked.

The man nodded. 'Spiral break of the tibia and fibula. Someone forgot to fill in a sitzmark. I was going pretty fast, and when I hit the hole . . .' He shrugged. 'I won't be able to walk without the crutches for at least another month.'

'That's too bad,' Hawes said. He paused, and then figured he might as well get down to business. 'I have a reservation,' he said. 'Adjoining rooms with bath.'

'Yes, sir. What was the name on that?'

'Cotton Hawes and Blanche Colby.'

The man opened a drawer in his desk and consulted a type-written sheet. 'Yes, sir,' he said. 'Two rooms in the annexe.'

'The annexe?' Hawes said. 'Where's that?'

'Oh, just a hundred yards or so from the main building, sir.'

'Oh. Well, I guess that'll be ...'

'And that's *one* bath, you understand.'

'What do you mean?'

'They're adjoining rooms, but the bathroom is in 104. 105 doesn't have a bath.'

'Oh. Well, I'd like two rooms that *do* have baths,' Hawes said, smiling.

'I'm sorry, sir. 104 and 105 are the only available rooms in the house.'

'The fellow I spoke to on the phone ...'

'Yes, sir, that's me. Elmer Wollender.'

'How do you do?' Hawes said. 'You told me both rooms had baths.'

'No, sir. You said you wanted adjoining rooms with bath, and I said I could give you adjoining rooms with bath. And that's what I've given you. Bath. Singular.'

'Are you a lawyer, Mr Wollender?' Hawes asked, no longer smiling.

'No, sir. Out of season, I'm a locksmith.'

'What are you in season?'

'Why, a hotel-keeper, sir,' Wollender said.

'Don't test the theory,' Hawes answered. 'Let me have my deposit back, Mr Wollender. We'll find another place to stay.'

'Well, sir, to begin with, we can't make any cash refunds, but we'll be happy to keep your deposit here against another time when you may wish ...'

'Look, Mr Wollender,' Hawes said menacingly, 'I don't know what kind of a ...'

'And of course, sir, there *are* lots of places to stay here in town, but none of **them**, sir, *none* of them have any private baths at all. Now if you don't mind walking down the hall ...'

'All I know is ...'

'... and sharing the john with a hundred other skiers, why then ...'

'You told me on the phone ...'

'I'm sure you can find other accommodations. The *lady*, however, might enjoy a little privacy.' Wollender waited while Hawes considered.

'If I give her 104 ...' Hawes started and then paused. 'Is that the room with the bath?'

'Yes, sir, 104.'

'If I give her that room, where's the bath for 105?'

'Down at the end of the hall, sir. And we *are* right at the base of the mountain, sir, and the skiing *has* been excellent, and we're expecting at least twelve inches of fresh powder.'

'The radio said four to six.'

'That's in the city, sir. We normally get a lot more snow.'

'Like what I got on the phone?' Hawes asked. 'Where do I sign?'

2

Cotton Hawes was a detective, and as a member of the 87th Squad he had flopped down in a great many desirable and un-desirable rooms throughout the city and its suburbs. Once, while posing as a dock walloper, he had taken a furnished room overlooking the River Harb, and had been surprised during the night by what sounded like a band of midgets marching at the foot of his bed. The midgets turned out to be giants, or at least giants of the species *Rattus muridae* – or as they say in English, rats. He had turned on the light and picked up a broom, but those brazen rat bastards had reared back on their hind legs like boxers and bared their teeth, and he was certain the pack of them would leap for his throat. He had checked out immediately.

There were no rats in rooms 104 and 105 of the annexe to Rawson Mountain Inn. Nor was there very much of anything else, either. Whoever had designed the accommodations was undoubtedly steeped in Spartan philosophy. The walls were white and bare, save for a single skiing poster over each bed. There was a single bed in each room, and a wooden dresser painted white. A portable cardboard clothes closet nestled in the corner of each room. The room Hawes hoped to occupy, the one without the bath, was excruciatingly hot, the vents sending in great waves of heated air. The room with the bath, Blanche's room, was unbearably cold. The single window was rimmed with frost, the floor was cold, the bed was cold, the heating ducts and vents were either clogged or blocked, but certainly inoperative.

'And *I'm* the one with the cold feet,' Blanche said.

'I'd let you have the heated room,' Hawes said gallantly, 'but this is the one with the bath.'

'Well, we'll manage,' Blanche said. 'Shall we go down for the bags?'

'I'll get them,' Hawes answered. 'Stay in my room for now, will you? There's no sense freezing in here.'

'I may get to like your room,' Blanche said archly, and then turned and walked past him through the connecting door.

He went down the long flight of steps to the front porch, and then beyond to where the car was parked. The rooms were over the ski shop, which was closed for the night now, silent and dark. He took the two valises out of the trunk, and then pulled his skis from the rack on top of the car. He was not a particularly distrustful man, but a pair of Head skis had been stolen from him the season before, and he'd been a cop long enough to know that lightning sometimes *did* strike twice in the same place. In his right hand, and under his right arm, he carried the two bags. In his left hand, and under his left arm, he carried his skis and his boots. He struggled through the deepening snow and on to the front porch. He was about to put down the bags in order to open the door when he heard the heavy thud of ski boots on the steps inside. Someone was coming down those steps in a hell of a hurry.

The door opened suddenly, and a tall thin man wearing black ski pants and a black-hooded parka came on to the porch, almost colliding with Hawes. His face was narrow, handsome in a fine-honed way, the sharply hooked nose giving it the edged striking appearance of an axe. Even in the pale light filtering from the hallway, Hawes saw that the man was deeply tanned, and automatically assumed he was an instructor. The guess was corroborated by the Rawson Mountain insignia on the man's right sleeve, an interlocking R and M in bright red letters. Incongruously, the man was carrying a pair of white figure skates in his left hand.

'Oh, I'm sorry,' he said. His face broke into a grin. He had spoken with an accent, German or Swedish, Hawes couldn't tell which.

'That's all right,' Hawes said.

'May I help you?'

'No, I think I can manage. If you'd just hold the door open for me ...'

'It will be my pleasure,' the man said, and he almost clicked his heels together.

'Has the skiing been good?' Hawes asked as he struggled through the narrow doorway.

'Fairly good,' the man answered. 'It will be better tomorrow.'

'Well, thanks,' Hawes said.

'My pleasure.'

'See you on the mountain,' Hawes said cheerfully and continued up the steps. There was something slightly ridiculous about the entire situation, the adjoining rooms with only one bath, the pristine cells the rooms had turned out to be, the heat in one, the cold in the other, the fact that they were over the ski shop, the fact that it had begun snowing very heavily, even the hurried ski instructor with his polite Teutonic manners and his guttural voice and his figure skates, there was something faintly reminiscent of farce about the whole set up. He began chuckling as he climbed the steps. When he came into his room, Blanche was stretched out on his bed. He put down the bags.

'What's so funny?' she asked.

'I've decided this is a comic-opera hotel,' Hawes said. 'I'll bet the mountain out there is only a backdrop. We'll go out there tomorrow morning and discover it's painted on canvas.'

'This room is nice and warm,' Blanche said.

'Yes, it is,' Hawes answered. He slid his skis under the bed, and she watched him silently.

'Are you expecting burglars?'

'You never can tell.' He took off his jacket and pulled his holstered service revolver from his back hip pocket.

'You going to wear that on the slopes tomorrow?' Blanche asked.

'No. You can't get a gun into those zippered pockets.'

'I think I'll stay in *this* room tonight,' Blanche said suddenly.

'Whatever you like,' Hawes said. 'I'll take the icebox next door.'

'Well, actually,' she said, 'that wasn't exactly what I had in mind.'

'Huh?'

'Don't detectives kiss people?'

'Huh?'

'We've been out twice together in the city, and we've just driven three hours alone together in a car, and you've never once tried to kiss me.'

'Well, I . . .'

'I wish you would,' Blanche said thoughtfully. 'Unless, of course, there's a department regulation against it.'

'None that I can think of,' Hawes said.

Blanche, her hands behind her head, her legs stretched luxuriously, suddenly took a deep breath and said, 'I think I'm going to like this place.'

3

There were sounds in the night.

Huddled together in the single bed, the first sound of which they were aware was the noise of the oil burner. At regularly spaced intervals, the thermostat would click, and there would be a thirty-second pause, and then a 707 jet aircraft would take off from the basement of the old wooden building. Hawes had never heard a noisier oil burner in his life. The aluminium ducts and vents provided a symphony all their own, too, expanding, contracting, banging, clanking, sighing, exhaling, whooshing. Down the hall, the toilet would be flushed every now and again, the noise sounding with cataract sharpness on the still mountain air.

There was another noise. A rasping sound, the narrow shrill squeak of metal upon metal. He got out of bed and went to the window. A light was burning in the ski shop below, casting a yellow rectangle on to the snow. Sighing, he went back to bed and tried to sleep.

Down the corridor, there was the constant thud of ski boots as guests returned to their rooms, the slamming of doors, the occasional high giggle of a girl skier intoxicated by the mountain air.

Voices.

'... will mean a slower track for the slalom ...'

'Sure, but everyone'll have the same handicap ...'

Fading.

More voices.

'... don't even think they'll open the upper trails.'

'They have to, don't they?'

'Not Dead Man's Fall. They won't even be able to get up there with all this snow. Seventeen inches already, and no end in sight.'

The 707 taking off again from the basement. The vents beginning their orchestral suite, the ducts supplying counterpoint. And more voices, raised in anger.

'... because he thinks he's God almighty!'

'I tell you you're imagining things.'

'I'm warning you! Stay away from him!'

A young girl's laughter.

'I'm warning you. If I see him ...'

Fading.

At two o'clock in the morning, the Cats started up the mountain. They sounded like Rommel's mechanized cavalry. Hawes was certain they would knock down the outside walls and come lumbering into the room. Blanche began giggling.

'This is the noisiest hotel I've ever slept in,' she said.

'How are your feet?'

'Nice and warm. You're a very warm man.'

'You're a very warm girl.'

'Do you mind my sleeping in long johns?'

'I thought they were leotards.'

'Leotard is singular,' Blanche said.

'Singular or plural, those are the sexiest long johns I've ever seen.'

'It's only the girl in them,' Blanche said modestly. 'Why don't you kiss me again?'

'I will. In a minute.'

'What are you listening for?'

'I thought I heard an unscheduled flight a moment ago.'

'What?'

'Didn't you hear it? A funny buzzing sound?'

'There are so many noises ...'

'Shhhh.'

They were silent for several moments. They could hear the Cats grinding their way up the mountain. Someone down the hall flushed the toilet. More boots in the corridor outside.

'Hey!' Blanche said.

'What?'

'You asleep?'

'No,' Hawes answered.

'That buzzing sound you heard?'

'Yes?'

'It was my blood,' she told him, and she kissed him on the mouth.

140

4

It was still snowing on Saturday morning. The promised storm had turned into a full-fledged blizzard. They dressed in the warm comfort of the room, Blanche putting on thermal underwear, and then two sweaters and stretch pants, the extra clothing padding out her slender figure. Hawes, standing six feet two inches tall in his double-stockinged feet, black pants and black sweater, presented a one-hundred-and-ninety-pound V-shaped silhouette to the window and the grey day outside.

'Do you think I'll get back in time for Monday night's rehearsal?' Blanche asked.

'I don't know. I'm supposed to be back at the squad by six tomorrow night. I wonder if the roads are open.'

They learned during breakfast that a state of emergency had been declared in the city and in most of the towns lining the upstate route. Blanche seemed blithely indifferent to the concept of being snowbound. 'If there's that much snow,' she said, 'they'll cancel the rehearsal, anyway.'

'They won't cancel the police department,' Hawes said.

'The hell with it,' Blanche said happily. 'We're here now, and there's marvellous snow, and if the skiing is good it'll be a wonderful weekend.'

'Even if the skiing is *lousy*,' Hawes said, 'it'll be a wonderful weekend.'

They rented boots and skis for her in the ski rental shop, and then took to the mountain. Both chair lifts were in operation, but as one of the midnight voices had prophesied, the upper trails were not yet opened. A strong wind had arisen, and it blew the snow in driving white sheets across the slopes. Hawes took Blanche to the rope tow first, had her practise climbing for a while, teaching her to edge and to herringbone, and then illustrated the use of the tow – left hand clamped around the rope, right hand and arm behind the back and gripping the rope. The beginners' slope was a gentle one, but Blanche seemed immediately capable of more difficult skiing. She was a trained dancer, and she automatically thought of the skis as part of a difficult stage costume, encumbering movement, but simply something to overcome. With remarkable coordination, she learned how to snowplough on the beginners' slope. By midmorning, she had graduated to the T-Bar, and was beginning to learn the rudiments of the stem christie. Hawes patiently stayed with her all morning, restricting his own skiing to the elementary slopes. He was becoming more and more grateful for the snow-clogged roads. With the roads impassable, the number of weekend skiers was limited; he and Blanche were enjoying weekday skiing on a Saturday, and the fresh snow made everything a delight.

After lunch, she suggested that he leave her alone to practise for a while. Hawes, who was itching to get at the chair lift and the real trails, nonetheless protested that he was perfectly content to ski with her on the baby slopes. But Blanche insisted, and he finally left her on the slope serviced by the T-Bar, and went to the longest of the chair lifts, Lift A.

He grinned unconsciously as he approached the lift. Eight or ten skiers were waiting to use the chairs, as compared to the long lines one usually encountered on weekends. As he approached the loading area, he caught a blur of black movement from the corner of his eye, turned and saw his German or Swedish ski instructor from the night before *wedeln* down the mountain, and then turning, parallel in a snow-spraying stop near the lift. He did not seem to recognize Hawes, but Hawes was not at all surprised. Every skier on the line was wearing a hooded parka, the hoods covering their heads and tied securely beneath their chins. In addition, all the skiers were wearing goggles, most with tinted yellow lenses in defence against the greyness of the day, some with darker lenses in spite of the greyness. The result, in any case, was almost total anonymity. Male and female, they all looked very much alike. They could have been a band of Martians waiting to be taken to a leader. Instead, they were waiting for chairs. They did not have to wait very long.

The chairs on their cable kept rounding the bend, came past

the grinding machinery. Hawes moved into position, watched the girl ahead of him sit abruptly as the chair came up under her behind. He noticed that the chair gave a decided lurch as it cleared the platform, and he braced himself for the expected force, glanced back over his shoulder as another chair rounded the turn. Ski poles clutched in his left hand, his right hand behind him to grip the edge of the chair as it approached, he waited. The chair was faster and had a stronger lurch than he'd anticipated. For a moment, he thought it would knock him down. He gripped the edge of the seat with his mittened right hand, felt himself sliding off the seat, and automatically grabbed for the upright supporting rod with his left hand, dropping his poles.

'Dropped your poles!' one of the loaders shouted behind him.

'We'll send them up!' the other loader called.

He turned slightly in the chair and looked back. He could see one of the loaders scrambling to pick up his poles. There were two empty chairs behind him, and then a skier got into the third chair, and the loader handed him the poles Hawes had dropped. Behind that chair, two other skiers shared a chair. The wind and the snow made it difficult to see. Hawes turned his head abruptly, but the wind was even stronger coming down the mountain. The chair ahead of him was perhaps thirty feet away, but he could barely make out the shadowy figure of the person sitting in it. All he saw was a dim silhouette obscured by blinding snow and keening wind. He could feel snow seeping under the edges of his hood. He took off his mittens and tightened the string. Quickly, before the biting cold numbed his fingers, he put the mittens on again.

The lift was a new one, and it pulled the chairs silently up the mountain. On his right, Hawes could see the skiers descending, a damn fool snowploughing out of control down a steep embankment pocked with moguls, an excellent skier navigating turns in parallel precision. The wind keened around and under his hood, the only sound on the mountain. The ride was a pleasant one, except for the wind and the cold. In some spots, the chair was suspended some thirty feet above the snow below. In other places, the chair came as close as six feet to the ground. He was beginning to anticipate the descent. He saw the unloading station ahead, saw the sign advising him to keep the tips of his skis up, and prepared to disembark. The skier ahead of him met with difficulty as he tried to get off his chair. The snow had been falling too heavily to clear, and there was no natural downgrade at the top of the lift; the chair followed its occupant, rather than rising overhead at the unloading point. The girl ahead of Hawes was almost knocked off her feet by her own chair. She managed to free herself as the chair gave a sharp lurch around the bend to begin its trip down the mountain again. Hawes concentrated on getting off the chair. Surprisingly, he did so with a minimum of effort and without poles, and then waited while the two empty chairs passed by. The third following chair approached the station. A man clambered off the chair, handed Hawes his poles with a 'These yours?' and skied to the crest of the slope. Hawes stood just outside the station booth, hanging his poles over his wrists. He was certain that the fourth chair behind his had contained *two* skiers at the bottom of the lift, and yet it seemed to be approaching now with only a single person in it. Hawes squinted through the snow, puzzled. Something seemed odd about the person in the fourth chair, something was jutting into the air at a curious angle – a ski? a leg? a ...?

The chair approached rapidly.

The skier made no move to disembark.

Hawes opened his eyes wide behind his yellow-tinted goggles as the chair swept past the station.

Through the driving snow, he had seen a skier slumped back into the passing chair, gloved hands dangling limply. And sticking out of the skier's chest at a malicious angle over the heart, buffeted by the wind and snow so that it trembled as if it were alive, thrust deep through the parka and the clothing beneath it like an oversized, slender aluminium sword, was a ski pole.

5

The chair gave its sharp lurch as it rounded the bend.

The skier slid from the seat as the chair made its abrupt turn. Skis touched snow, the body fell forward, there was a terrible snapping sound over the keening of the wind, and Hawes knew instantly that a leg had been broken as bone yielded to the unresisting laminated wood and the vicelike binding. The skier fell face downwards, the ski pole bending as the body struck the snow, one leg twisted at an impossible angle, the boot still held firmly in its binding.

For a moment, there was only confusion compounded.

The wind and the snow filled the air, the body lay motionless, face down in the snow as the chair whipped around the turn and started its descent. An empty chair swept past, another, a third, and then a chair came into view with a man poised to disembark, and Hawes shouted to the booth attendant, 'Stop the lift!'

'What?'

'Stop the goddamn lift!'

'What? What?'

Hawes moved towards the body lying in the snow just as the man on the chair decided to get off. They collided in a tangle of poles and skis, the relentless chair pushing them along like a bulldozer, sending them sprawling on to the body in the snow, before it snapped around for its downward passage. The booth attendant finally got the message. He ran into the small wooden shack and threw the control switch. The lift stopped. There was a deeper silence on the mountain.

'You okay?' he called.

'I'm fine,' Hawes said. He got to his feet and quickly unsnapped his bindings. The man who'd knocked him down was apologizing profusely, but Hawes wasn't listening. There was a bright red stain spreading into the snow where the impaled skier had fallen. He turned the body over and saw the ashen face and sightless eyes, saw the blood-soaked parka where the

145

pole had been pushed through the soft and curving breast into the heart.

The dead skier was a young girl, no more than nineteen years old.

On the right sleeve of her black parka was the insignia of a Rawson Mountain ski instructor, the interlocking R and M in red as bright as the blood which seeped into the thirsty snow.

'What is it?' the booth attendant shouted. 'Shall I get the ski patrol? Is it an accident?'

'It's no accident,' Hawes said, but his voice was so low that no one heard him.

6

As befitted this farcical hotel in this comic-opera town, the police were a band of Keystone cops led by an inept sheriff who worked on the premise that a thing worth doing was a thing worth doing badly. Hawes stood by helplessly as he watched these cracker-barrel cops violate each and every rule of investigation, watched as they mishandled evidence, watched as they made it hopelessly impossible to gain any information at all from whatever slender clues were available.

The sheriff was a gangling oaf named Theodore Watt who, instead of putting Lift A out of commission instantly while his men tried to locate the victim's chair, instead rode that very lift to the top of the mountain, followed by at least three dozen skiers, hotel officials, reporters, and local cretins who undoubtedly smeared any latent prints lingering on *any* of the chairs, and made the task of reconstructing the crime almost impossible. One girl, wearing bright lavender stretch pants and a white parka, climbed off the chair near the booth and was promptly informed there was blood all over the seat of her pants. The girl craned her neck to examine her shapely behind, touched the smear of blood, decided it was sticky and obscene, and almost fainted dead away. The chair, meantime, was happily whisking its way down the mountain again to the loading station where, presumably, another skier would again sit into a puddle of the dead girl's blood.

The dead girl's name, as it turned out, was Helga Nilson. She was nineteen years old and had learned to ski before she'd learned to walk, as the old Swedish saying goes. She had come to America when she was fifteen, had taught in the ski school at Stowe, Vermont, for two years before moving down to Mt Snow in that same fair state, and then abandoning Vermont and moving to Rawson Mountain, further south. She had joined the Rawson ski school at the beginning of the season, and seemed to be well-liked by all the instructors and especially by many beginning skiers who, after one lesson with her, repeatedly asked for 'Helga, the little Swedish girl'.

The little Swedish girl had had a ski pole driven into her heart with such force that it had almost exited through her back. The pole, bent out of shape when Helga fell from the chair, was the first piece of real evidence that the Keystone cops mishandled. Hawes saw one of the deputies kneel down beside the dead girl, grasp the pole with both hands, and attempt to pull it out of her body.

'Hey, what are you doing?' he shouted, and he shoved the man away from the body.

The man glanced up at him with a baleful upstate eye. 'And just who in hell're *you*?' he asked.

'My name's Cotton Hawes,' Hawes said. 'I'm a detective. From the city.' He unzipped the left hip pocket of his ski pants, pulled out his wallet, and flashed the tin. The deputy seemed singularly unimpressed.

'You're a little bit aways from your jurisdiction, ain't you?' he said.

'Who taught you how to handle evidence?' Hawes asked heatedly.

Sheriff Watt sauntered over to where the pair were arguing.

He grinned amiably and said, 'What seems to be the trouble here, hmmm?' He sang out the 'hmmm', his voice rising pleasantly and cheerfully. A nineteen-year-old girl lay dead at his feet, but Sheriff Watt thought he was an old alumnus at Dartmouth's Winter Carnival.

'Feller here's a city detective,' the deputy said.

'That's good,' Watt said. 'Pleased to have you with us.'

'Thanks,' Hawes said. 'Your man here was just smearing any latent prints there may be on that weapon.'

'What weapon?'

'The ski pole,' Hawes said. 'What weapon do you think I ...?'

'Oh, won't be no fingerprints on that, anyway,' Watt said.

'How do you know?'

'No damn fool's gonna grab a piece of metal with his bare hands, is he? Not when the temperature's ten below zero, now is he?'

'He might have,' Hawes said. 'And while we're at it, don't you think it'd be a good idea to stop that lift? You've already had one person smearing up whatever stuff you could have found in the ...'

'I got to get my men up here before I order the lift stopped,' Watt said.

'Then restrict it to the use of your men.'

'I've already done that,' Watt said briefly. He turned back to his deputy. 'Want to let me see that pole, Fred?'

'Sheriff, you let him touch that pole again, and—'

'And *what*?'

'—and you may ruin—'

'Mister, you just let me handle this my own whichway, hmmm? We been in this business a long time now, and we know all about skiing accidents.'

'This wasn't an accident,' Hawes said angrily. 'Somebody shoved a ski pole into that girl's chest, and that's not ...'

'I know it wasn't an accident,' Watt said. 'That was just a manner of speaking. Let me have the pole, Fred.'

'Sheriff ...'

'Mister, you better just shut up, hmmm? Else I'll have one

148

of my men escort you down the mountain, and you can warm your feet by the fire.'

Hawes shut up. Impotently, he watched while the deputy named Fred seized the ski pole in both hands and yanked it from Helga's chest. A spurt of blood followed the retreating pole, welled up into the open wound, overflowed it, was sopped up by the sodden sweater. Fred handed the bent pole to the sheriff. Watt turned it over and over in his big hands.

'Looks like the basket's been taken off this thing,' he said.

The basket, Hawes saw, had indeed been removed from the bottom of the aluminium pole. The basket on a ski pole is a circular metal ring perhaps five inches in diameter, crossed by a pair of leather thongs. A smaller ring stamped into the thongs fits over the end of the pointed pole and is usually fastened by a cotter pin or a tight rubber washer. When the basket is in place on the end of a pole, it prevents the pole from sinking into the snow, thereby enabling the skier to use it in executing turns or maintaining balance. The basket had been removed from this particular pole and, in addition, someone had sharpened the normally sharp point so that it was as thin as a rapier. Hawes noticed this at once. It took the sheriff a little while longer to see that he was holding a razor-sharp weapon in his hands, and not a normally pointed pole.

'Somebody been working on the end of this thing,' he said, the dawn gradually breaking.

A doctor had come up the lift and was kneeling beside the dead girl. To no one's particular surprise, he pronounced her dead. One of the sheriff's bumbling associates began marking the position of the body, tracing its outline on the snow with a blue powder he poured liberally from a can.

Hawes couldn't imagine what possible use this imitation of investigatory technique would serve. They were marking the position of the body, true, but this didn't happen to be the scene of the crime. The girl had been murdered on a chair somewhere between the base of the mountain and the top of the lift. So far, no one had made any attempt to locate and examine the chair. Instead, they were sprinkling blue powder on to the snow, and passing their big paws all over the murder weapon.

'May I make a suggestion?' he asked.

'Sure,' Watt said.

'That girl got on the lift with someone else. I know because I dropped my poles down there, and when I turned for a look, there were two people in that chair. But when she reached the station here, she was alone.'

'Yeah?' Watt said.

'Yeah. I suggest you talk to the loader down below. The girl was a ski instructor, and they may have recognized her. Maybe they know who got on the chair with her.'

'Provided anyone did.'

'Someone did,' Hawes said.

'How do you know?'

'Because . . .' Hawes took a deep breath. 'I just told you. I *saw* two people in that chair.'

'How far behind you?'

'Four chairs behind.'

'And you could see four chairs behind you in this storm, hmmm?'

'Yes. Not clearly, but I could see.'

'I'll just bet you could,' Watt said.

'Look,' Hawes insisted, 'someone was in that chair with her. And he undoubtedly jumped from the chair right after he killed her. I suggest you start combing the ground under the lift before this snow covers any tracks that might be there.'

'Yes, we'll do that,' Watt said. 'When we get around to it.'

'You'd better get around to it soon,' Hawes said. 'You've got a blizzard here, and a strong wind piling up drifts. If . . .'

'Mister, I hadn't *better* do anything. You're the one who'd just better butt his nose out of what we're trying to do here.'

'What is it you're trying to do?' Hawes asked. 'Compound a felony? Do you think your murderer's going to sit around and wait for you to catch up to him? He's probably halfway out of the state by now.'

'Ain't nobody going noplace, mister,' Watt said. 'Not with

the condition of the roads. So don't you worry about that. I hate to see anybody worrying.'

'Tell that to the dead girl,' Hawes said, and he watched as the ski patrol loaded her into a basket and began taking her on her last trip down the mountain.

7

Death is a cliché, a tired old saw.

He had been a cop for a good long time now, starting as a rookie who saw death only from the sidelines, who kept a timetable while the detectives and the photographers and the assistant ME and the laboratory boys swarmed around the victim like flies around a prime cut of rotten meat. Death to him, at that time, had been motion-picture death. Standing apart from death, being as it were a uniformed secretary who took the names of witnesses and jotted in a black book the arrivals and departures of those actually concerned with the investigation, he had watched the proceedings dispassionately. The person lying lifeless on the sidewalk, the person lying on blood-soaked sheets, the person hanging from a light fixture, the person eviscerated by the onrushing front grille of an automobile, these were all a trifle unreal to Hawes, representations of death, but not death itself, not that grisly son of a bitch.

When he became a detective, they really introduced him to death.

The introduction was informal, almost casual. He was working with the 30th Squad at the time, a very nice respectable squad in a nice respectable precinct where death by violence hardly ever came. The introduction was made in a rooming house. The patrolman who answered the initial squeal was waiting for the detectives when they had arrived. The detective with Hawes asked, 'Where's the stiff?' and the patrolman answered, 'He's in there,' and the other detective turned to Hawes and said, 'Come on, let's take a look.'

That was the introduction.

They had gone into the bedroom where the man was lying at the foot of the dresser. The man was fifty-three years old. He lay in his undershorts on the floor in the sticky coagulation of his own blood. He was a small man with a pinched chest. His hair was black and thinning, and bald patches showed his flaking scalp. He had probably never been handsome, even when he was a youth. Some men do not improve with age, and time and alcohol had squeezed everything out of this man, and drained him dry until all he possessed was sagging flesh and, of course, life. The flesh was still there. The life had been taken from him. He lay at the foot of the dresser in his undershorts, ludicrously piled into a heap of inert flesh, so relaxed, so impossibly relaxed. Someone had worked him over with a hatchet. The hatchet was still in the room, blood-flecked, entangled with thin black hair. The killer had viciously attacked him around the head and the throat and the chest. He had stopped bleeding by the time they arrived, but the wounds were still there to see, open and raw.

Hawes vomited.

He went into the bathroom and vomited. That was his introduction to death.

He had seen a lot of death since, had come close to being dead himself. The closest, perhaps, was the time he'd been stabbed while investigating a burglary. The woman who'd been burglarized was still pretty hysterical when he got there. He asked his questions and tried to comfort her, and then started downstairs to get a patrolman. The woman, terrified, began screaming when he left. He could hear her screams as he went down the stairwell. The superintendent of the building caught him on the second floor landing. He was carrying a bread knife, and he thought that Hawes was the burglar returned, and he stabbed repeatedly at his head, ripping a wound over his left temple before Hawes finally subdued him. They let the super go; the poor guy had actually thought Hawes was the thief. And then they'd shaved Hawes' red hair to get to the wound, which time of course healed as it does all wounds, leaving however a reminder of death, of the closeness of death. The red hair had grown white. He still carried the streak over his temple. Sometimes, particularly when it rained, death sent little signals of pain to accompany the new hair.

He had seen a lot of death, especially since he'd joined the 87th, and a lot of dying. He no longer vomited. The vomiting had happened to a very young Cotton Hawes, a very young and innocent cop who suddenly awoke to the knowledge that he was in a dirty business where the facts of life were the facts of violence, where he dealt daily with the sordid and grotesque. He no longer vomited. But he still got angry.

He had felt anger on the mountain when the young girl fell out of the chair and struck the snow, the ski pole bending as she dropped into that ludicrously ridiculous posture of the dead, that totally relaxed and utterly frightening posture. He had felt anger by juxtaposition, the reconstruction of a vibrant and life-bursting athlete against the very real image of the same girl, no longer a girl, only a worthless heap of flesh and bones, only a body now, a corpse. 'Where's the stiff?'

He felt anger when Theodore Watt and his witless assistants muddied the residue of sudden death, allowing the killer a precious edge, presenting him with the opportunity for escape – escape from the law and from the outrage of humanity. He felt anger now as he walked back to the building which housed the ski shop and the rooms overhead.

The anger seemed out of place on the silent mountain. The snow still fell, still and gentle. The wind had died, and now the flakes drifted aimlessly from overhead, large and wet and white, and there was a stillness and a peace to Rawson Mountain and the countryside beyond, a lazy white quiet which denied the presence of death.

He kicked the packed snow from his boots and went up the steps.

He was starting down the corridor towards his room when he noticed the door was slightly ajar. He hesitated. Perhaps Blanche had come back to the room, perhaps ...

But there was silence in the corridor, a silence as large as noise. He stooped and untied the laces on his boots. Gently, he slipped them from his feet. Walking as softly as he could – he was a big man and the floor boards in the old building creaked beneath his weight – he approached the room. He did not like the idea of being in his stockinged feet. He had had to kick men too often, and he knew the value of shoes. He hesitated just outside the door. There was no sound in the room. The door was open no more than three inches. He put his hand against the wood. Somewhere in the basement, the oil burner clicked and then *whoooomed* into action. He shoved open the door.

Elmer Wollender, his crutches under his arms, whirled to face him. His head had been bent in an attitude of ... prayer, was it? No. Not prayer. He had been listening, that was it, listening *to* something, or *for* something.

'Oh, hello, Mr Hawes,' he said. He was wearing a red ski parka over his white shirt. He leaned on his crutches and grinned a boyish, disarming grin.

'Hello, Mr Wollender,' Hawes said. 'Would you mind telling me, Mr Wollender, just what the hell you're doing in my room?'

Wollender seemed surprised. His eyebrows arched. He tilted his head to one side, almost in admiration, almost as if he too would have behaved in much the same way had he come back to *his* room and found a stranger in it. But the admiration was also tinged with surprise. This was obviously a mistake. Head cocked to one side, eyebrows arched, the boyish smile on his mouth, Wollender leaned on his crutches and prepared to explain. Hawes waited.

'You said the heat wasn't working, didn't you?' Wollender said. 'I was just checking it.'

'The heat's working fine in this room,' Hawes said. 'It's the room next door.'

'Oh.' Wollender nodded. 'Oh, is that it?'

'That's it, yes.'

'No wonder. I stuck my hand up there to check the vent, and it seemed fine to me.'

'Yes, it would be fine,' Hawes said, 'since there was never anything wrong with it. I told you at the desk this morning that the heat wasn't working in 104. This is 105. Are you new here, Mr Wollender?'

'I guess I misunderstood you.'

'Yes, I guess so. Misunderstanding isn't a wise practice, Mr Wollender, especially with your local cops crawling all over the mountain.'

'What are you talking about?'

'I'm talking about the girl. When those imitation cops begin asking questions, I suggest ...'

'What girl?'

Hawes looked at Wollender for a long time. The question on Wollender's face and in his eyes looked genuine enough, but could there possibly be someone on the mountain who still had not heard of the murder? Was it possible that Wollender, who ran the inn, the centre of all activity and gossip, did not know Helga Nilson was dead?

'The girl,' Hawes said. 'Helga Nilson.'

'What about her?'

Hawes knew enough about baseball to realize you didn't throw your fast ball until you'd tried a few curves. 'Do you know her?' he asked.

'Of course, I know her. I know all the ski instructors. She rooms right here, down the hall.'

'Who else rooms here?'

'Why?'

'I want to know.'

'Just her and Maria,' Wollender said. 'Maria Fiers. She's an instructor, too. And, oh yes, the new man. Larry Davidson.'

'Is he an instructor?' Hawes asked. 'About this tall?'

'Yes.'

'Hooked nose? German accent.'

'No, no. You're thinking of Helmut Kurtz. And that's an

155

Austrian accent.' Wollender paused. 'Why? Why do you want to ...?'

'Anything between him and Helga?'

'Why, no. Not that I know of. They teach together, but ...'

'What about Davidson?'

'Larry Davidson?'

'Yes.'

'Do you mean, is he dating Helga, or ...'

'Yes, that's right.'

'Larry's married,' Wollender said. 'I would hardly think ...'

'What about you?'

'I don't understand.'

'You and Helga. Anything?'

'Helga's a good friend of mine,' Wollender said.

'Was,' Hawes corrected.

'Huh?'

'She's dead. She was killed on the mountain this afternoon.'

There was the fast ball, and it took Wollender smack between the eyes. 'Dea—' he started, and then his jaw fell slack, and his eyes went blank. He staggered back a pace, colliding with the white dresser. The crutches dropped from his hands. He struggled to maintain his balance, the leg with the cast stiff and unwieldy; he seemed about to fall. Hawes grabbed at his elbow and pulled him erect. He stooped down for Wollender's crutches and handed them to him. Wollender was still dazed. He groped for the crutches, fumbled, dropped them again. Hawes picked them up a second time, and forced them under Wollender's arms. Wollender leaned back against the dresser. He kept staring at the wall opposite, where a poster advertising the pleasures of Kitzbühel was hanging.

'She ... she took too many chances,' he said. 'She always went too fast. I told her ...'

'This wasn't a skiing accident,' Hawes said. 'She was murdered.'

'No.' Wollender shook his head. 'No.'

'Yes.'

'No. Everyone liked Helga. No one would ...' He kept

shaking his head. His eyes stayed riveted to the Kitzbühel poster.

'There are going to be cops here, Mr Wollender,' Hawes said. 'You seem like a nice kid. When they start asking questions, you'd better have a more plausible story than the one you invented about being in my room. They're not going to fool around. They're looking for a killer.'

'Why ... why do you *think* I came here?' Wollender asked.

'I don't know. Maybe you were looking for some pocket money. Skiers often leave their wallets and their valu—'

'I'm not a thief, Mr Hawes,' Wollender said with dignity. 'I only came here to give you some heat.'

'That makes it even,' Hawes answered. 'The cops'll be coming here to give *you* some.'

8

He found the two loaders in the lodge cafeteria. The lifts had been closed at four-thirty, the area management having reached the conclusion that most skiing accidents took place in the waning hours of the afternoon, when poor visibility and physical exhaustion combined to create gentle havoc. They were both burly, grizzled men wearing Mackinaws, their thick hands curled around coffee mugs. They had been loading skiers on to chairs ever since the area was opened, and they worked well together as a team. Even their dialogue seemed concocted in one mind, though it issued from two mouths.

'My name's Jake,' the first loader said. 'This here is Obey, short for Obadiah.'

'Only I ain't so short,' Obadiah said.

'He's short on brains,' Jake said and grinned. Obadiah returned the grin. 'You're a cop, huh?'

'Yes,' Hawes said. He had shown them his buzzer the moment he approached them. He had also told an outright lie, saying he was helping with the investigation of the case, having been sent up from the city because there was the possibility a known and wanted criminal had perpetrated the crime, confusing his own doubletalk as he wove a fantastic monologue which Jake and Obadiah seemed to accept.

'And you want to know who we loaded on them chairs, right? Same as Teddy wanted to know.'

'Teddy?'

'Teddy Watt. The sheriff.'

'Oh. Yes,' Hawes said. 'That's right.'

'Whyn't you just ask *him*?' Obadiah said.

'Well, I have,' Hawes lied. 'But sometimes a fresh angle will come up if witnesses can be questioned directly, do you see?'

'Well, we ain't exactly witnesses,' Jake said. 'We didn't see her get killed, you know.'

'Yes, but you did load her on the chair, didn't you?'

'That's right. We did, all right.'

'And someone was in the chair with her, is that right?'

'That's right,' Jake said.

'Who?' Hawes asked.

'Seems like everybody wants to know *who*,' Jake said.

'Ain't it the damndest thing?' Obadiah said.

'Do you remember?' Hawes asked.

'We remember it was snowing, that's for sure.'

'Couldn't hardly see the chairs, it was snowing that hard.'

'Pretty tough to reckernize one skier from another with all that wind and snow, wouldn't you say, Obey?'

'Next to impossible,' Obadiah answered.

'But you did recognize Helga,' Hawes suggested.

'Oh, sure. But she said hello to us, you see. She said, "Hello, Jake. Hello, Obey." And also, she took the chair closest to the loading platform, the inside chair. The guy took the other chair.'

'Guy?' Hawes asked. 'It was a man then? The person who took the chair next to her was a man?'

'Well, can't say for sure,' Jake said. 'Was a time when men's

158

ski clothes was different from the ladies', but that don't hold true no more.'

'Not by a long shot,' Obadiah said.

'Nowadays, you find yourself following some pretty girl in purple pants, she turns out to be a man. It ain't so easy to tell them apart no more.'

'Then you don't know whether the person who sat next to her was a man or a woman, is that right?' Hawes asked.

'That's right.'

'Coulda been either.'

'Did this person say anything?'

'Not a word.'

'What was he wearing?'

'Well, we ain't established it was a *he*,' Jake reminded him.

'Yes, I know. I meant the ... the person who took the chair. It'll be easier if we give him a gender.'

'Give him a *what*?'

'A gen— if we assume for the moment that the person was a man.'

'Oh.' Jake thought this over. 'Okay, if you say so. Seems like pretty sloppy deduction to me, though.'

'Well, I'm not actually making a deduction. I'm simply trying to facilitate ...'

'Sure, I understand,' Jake said. 'But it's sure pretty sloppy.'

Hawes sighed. 'Well ... what *was* he wearing?'

'Black,' Jake said.

'Black ski pants, black parka,' Obadiah said.

'Any hat?' Hawes asked.

'Nope. Hood on the parka was pulled clear up over the head. Sunglasses over the eyes.'

'Gloves or mittens?' Hawes asked.

'Gloves. Black gloves.'

'Did you notice whether or not there was an insignia on the man's parka?'

'What kind of insignia?'

'An R-M interlocked,' Hawes said.

'Like the instructors wear?' Jake asked.

'Exactly.'

'They wear it on their *right* sleeves,' Obadiah said. 'We told you this person took the outside chair. We couldn'ta seen the right sleeve, even if there *was* anything on it.'

Hawes suddenly had a wild idea. He hesitated before he asked, and then thought, *What the hell, try it.*

'This person,' he said, 'was he ... was he carrying crutches?'

'Carrying *what*?' Jake asked incredulously.

'Crutches. Was his leg in a cast?'

'Now how in hell ... of *course* not,' Jake said. 'He was wearing skis and he was carrying ski poles. Crutches and a cast! My God! It's hard enough getting on that damn lift as it is. Can you just picture ...'

'Never mind,' Hawes said. 'Forget it. Did this person say anything to Helga?'

'Not a word.'

'Did she say anything to him?'

'Nothing we could hear. The wind was blowing pretty fierce.'

'But you heard her when she said hello to you.'

'That's right.'

'Then if she'd said anything to this person, you might have heard that, too.'

'That's right. We didn't hear nothing.'

'You said he was carrying poles. Did you notice anything unusual about the poles?'

'Seemed like ordinary poles to me,' Jake said.

'Did both poles have baskets?'

Jake shrugged. 'I didn't notice. Did you, Obey?'

'Both seemed to have baskets,' Obadiah said. 'Who'd notice a thing like that?'

'Well, you might have,' Hawes said. 'If there'd been anything unusual, you might have noticed.'

'I didn't notice nothing unusual,' Obadiah said. 'Except I thought to myself this feller must be pretty cold.'

'Why?'

'Well, the hood pulled up over his head, and the scarf wrapped almost clear around his face.'

'What scarf? You didn't mention that before.'

160

'Sure. He was wearing a red scarf. Covered his mouth and his nose, reached right up to the sunglasses.'

'Hmmm,' Hawes said, and the table went still.

'You're the fellow dropped his poles on the way up, ain't you?' Jake asked.

'Yes.'

'Thought I remembered you.'

'If you remember *me*, how come you can't remember the person who took that chair alongside Helga's?'

'You saying I *should*, mister?'

'I'm only asking.'

'Well, like maybe if I seen a guy wearing black pants and a black hood, and sunglasses, and a scarf wrapped clear around his face, why maybe then I would recognize him. But, the way I figure it, he ain't likely to be wearing the same clothes right now, is he?'

'I don't suppose so,' Hawes said, sighing.

'Yeah, neither do I,' Jake answered. 'And I ain't even a cop.'

9

Dusk was settling upon the mountain.

It spread into the sky and stained the snow a purple-red. The storm was beginning to taper off, the clouds vanishing before the final triumphant breakthrough of the setting sun. There was an unimaginable hush to the mountain, and the town, and the valley beyond, a hush broken only by the sound of gently jingling skid-chains on hard-packed snow.

He had found Blanche and taken her to the fireplace in the inn, settling her there with a brace of double Scotches and a

161

half-dozen copies of a skiing magazine. Now, with the mountain and the town still, the lifts inoperative, the distant snow brushed with dying colour, he started climbing the mountain. He worked through the deep snow directly under the lift, the chairs hanging motionless over his head. He was wearing ski pants and after-ski boots designed for lounging beside a fire. He had forsaken his light parka for two sweaters. Before he'd left the room, he had unholstered the .38 and slipped it into the elastic-reinforced waistband of his trousers. He could feel it digging into his abdomen now as he climbed.

The climb was not an easy one.

The snow under the lift had not been packed, and he struggled against it as he climbed, encountering drifts which were impassable, working his way in a zigzagging manner across the lift line, sometimes being forced to leave the high snow for the Cat-packed trail to the right of the lift. The light was waning. He did not know how much longer it would last. He had taken a flashlight from the glove compartment of his car, but he began to wonder whether its glow would illuminate very much once the sun had set. He began to wonder, too, exactly what he hoped to find. He was almost certain that any tracks the killer had left would already have been covered by the drifting snow. Again he cursed Theodore Watt and his inefficient slobs. Someone should have made this climb immediately after they discovered the dead girl, while there was still a possibility of finding a trail.

He continued climbing. After a day of skiing, he was physically and mentally exhausted, his muscles protesting, his eyes burning. He thumbed on the flashlight as darkness claimed the mountain, and pushed his way through knee-deep snow. He stumbled and got to his feet again. The snow had tapered almost completely, but the wind had returned with early evening, a high keening wind that rushed through the trees on either side of the lift line, pushing the clouds from the sky. There was a thin sliver of moon and a scattering of stars. The clouds raced past them like silent dark horsemen, and everywhere on the mountain was the piercing shriek of the wind, a thin scream that penetrated to the marrow.

He fell again.

Loose snow caught under the neck of his sweater, slid down his back. He shivered and tried to brush it away, got to his feet, and doggedly began climbing again. His after-ski boots had not been designed for deep snow. The tops ended just above his ankles, offering no protection whatever. He realized abruptly that the boots were already packed with snow, that his feet were literally encased in snow. He was beginning to regret this whole foolhardy mission, when he saw it.

He had come perhaps a third of the way up the lift line, the mountain in absolute darkness now, still except for the maiden scream of the wind. The flashlight played a small circle of light on the snow ahead of him as he stumbled upwards, the climb more difficult now, the clouds rushing by overhead, skirting the thin moon. The light touched something which glinted momentarily, passed on as he continued climbing, stopped. He swung the flashlight back. Whatever had glinted was no longer there. Swearing, he swung the flashlight in a slow steady arc. The glint again. He swung the light back.

The basket was half-covered by the snow. Only one edge of its metallic ring showed in the beam of his light. It had probably been covered completely earlier in the day, but the strong fresh wind had exposed it to view again, and he stooped quickly to pick it up, almost as if he were afraid it would vanish. He was still bending, studying the basket in the light of the flash, when the man jumped on to his back.

The attack came suddenly and swiftly. He had heard nothing but the wind. He had been so occupied with his find, so intent on studying the basket which, he was certain, had come from the end of the ski pole weapon, and when he felt the sudden weight on his back he did not connect it immediately with an attack. He was simply surprised, and his first thought was that one of the pines had dropped a heavy load of snow from its laden branches, and then he realized this was no heavy load of snow, but by that time he was flat on his belly.

He rolled over instantly. He held the ski pole basket in his left hand, refusing to let go of it. In his right hand, he held the flashlight, and he swung that instantly at the man's head, felt it hitting the man's forearm instead. Something solid struck Hawes' shoulder; a wrench? a hammer? and he realized at once that the man was armed, and suddenly the situation became serious. He threw away the flashlight and groped for the .38 in his waistband.

The clouds cleared the moon. The figure kneeling over him, straddling him, was wearing a black parka, the hood pulled up over his head. A red scarf was wrapped over his chin and his mouth and his nose. He was holding a hammer in his right hand, and he raised the hammer over his head just as the moon disappeared again. Hawes' fingers closed on the butt of the .38. The hammer descended.

It descended in darkness, striking Hawes on his cheek, ripping the flesh, glancing downwards and catching his shoulder. Hawes swore violently, drew the .38 in a ridiculously clumsy draw, brought it into firing position, and felt again the driving blow of the other man's weapon, the hammer lashing out of the darkness, slamming with brute force against his wrist, almost cracking the bone. His fingers opened involuntarily. The gun dropped into the snow. He bellowed in pain and tried to kick out at his attacker, but the man moved away quickly, gained his feet, and braced himself in the deep snow for the final assault. The moon appeared again. A thin silvery light put the man in silhouette against the sky, the black hooded head, the face masked by a scarf. The hammer went up over his head.

Hawes kicked out at his groin.

The blow did nothing to stop the man's attack. It glanced off his thigh, missing target as the hammer came down, but throwing him off balance slightly so that the hammer struck without real force. Hawes threw a fist at him, and the man grunted and again the hammer came out of the new darkness. The man fought desperately and silently, frightening Hawes with the fury of his animal strength. They rolled over in the snow, and Hawes grasped at the hood, tried to pull it from the man's head, found it was securely tied in place, and reached for the scarf. The scarf began to unravel. The man lashed out with the hammer, felt the scarf coming free, pulled back to avoid exposing his face, and suddenly staggered as Hawes' fist struck home. He fell into the snow, and all at once, he panicked. Instead of attacking again, he pulled the scarf around his face and began to half run, half stumble through the deep snow. Hawes leaped at him, missing, his hands grabbing air. The man scrambled over the snow, heading for the pines lining the lift. By the times Hawes was on his feet again, the man had gone into the trees. Hawes went after him. It was dark under the trees. The world went black and silent under the pines.

He hesitated for a moment. He could see nothing, could hear nothing. He fully expected the hammer to come lashing out of the darkness.

Instead, there came the voice.

'Hold it right there.'

The voice startled him, but he reacted intuitively, whirling, his fist pulling back reflexively, and then firing into the darkness. He felt it connecting with solid flesh, heard someone swearing in the dark, and then – surprisingly, shockingly – Hawes heard the sound of a pistol shot. It rang on the mountain air, reverberated under the pines. Hawes opened his eyes wide. A pistol? But the man had only a hammer. Why hadn't ...?

'Next time, I go for your heart,' the voice said.

Hawes stared into the darkness. He could no longer locate the voice. He did not know where to jump, and the man was holding a pistol.

'You finished?' the man asked.

The beam of a flashlight suddenly stabbed through the darkness. Hawes blinked his eyes against it, tried to shield his face.

'Well, well,' the man said. 'You never can tell, can you? Stick out your hands.'

'What?' Hawes said.

'Stick out your goddamn hands.'

Hesitantly he held out his hands. He was the most sur-

prised human being in the world when he felt the handcuffs
being snapped on to his wrists.

10

The office from which Theodore Watt, sheriff of the town of
Rawson, operated was on the main street alongside an Italian
restaurant whose neon sign advertised LASAGNA * SPAGHETTI *
RAVIOLI. Now that the snow had stopped, the ploughs had
come through and banked snow on either side of the road so
that the door of the office was partially hidden by a natural
fortress of white. Inside the office, Theodore Watt was partially hidden by the fortress of his desk, the top of which was
covered with Wanted circulars, FBI flyers, carbon copies of
police reports, a pair of manacles, a cardboard container of
coffee, a half-dozen chewed pencil stubs, and a framed picture
of his wife and three children. Theodore Watt was not in a
very friendly mood. He sat behind his desk-fortress, a frown
on his face. Cotton Hawes stood before the desk, still wearing
the handcuffs which had been clamped on to his wrists on the
mountain. The deputy who'd made the collar, the self-same
Fred who had earlier pulled the ski pole from Helga Nilson's
chest, stood alongside Hawes, wearing the sheriff's frown,
and also wearing a mouse under his left eye, where Hawes
had hit him.

'I could lock you up, you know,' Watt said, frowning. 'You
hit one of my deputies.'

'You ought to lock *him* up,' Hawes said angrily. 'If he
hadn't come along, I might have had our man.'

'You might have, huh?'

'Yes.'

'You had no right being on that damn mountain,' Watt said. 'What were you doing up there?'

'Looking.'

'For what?'

'Anything. He gave you the basket I found. Apparently it was important enough for the killer to have wanted it, too. He fought hard enough for it. Look at my cheek.'

'Well now, that's a shame,' Watt said drily.

'There may be fingerprints on that basket,' Hawes said. 'I suggest . . .'

'I doubt it. Weren't none on the ski pole, and none on the chair, neither. We talked to the two loaders, and they told us the one riding up with Helga Nilson was wearing gloves. I doubt if there's any fingerprints on that basket at all.'

'Well . . .' Hawes said, and he shrugged.

'What it amounts to, hmmmm,' Watt said, 'is that you figured we wasn't handling this case to your satisfaction, ain't that it? So you figured you'd give us local hicks a little bigtime help, hmmmm? Ain't that about it?'

'I thought I could possibly assist in some . . .'

'Then you shoulda come to me,' Watt said, 'and *asked* if you could help. This way, you only fouled up what we was trying to do.'

'I don't understand.'

'I've got six men on that mountain,' Watt said, 'waiting for whoever killed that girl to come back and cover his mistakes. This basket here was one of the mistakes. But did our killer find it? No. Our helpful big-city detective found it. You're a lot of help, mister, you sure are. With all that ruckus on the mountain, that damn killer won't go anywhere near it for a month!'

'I almost had him,' Hawes said. 'I was going after him when your man stopped me.'

'Stopped him, hell! *You're* the one who was stopping *him* from doing his job. Maybe I *ought* to lock you up. There's a thing known as impeding the progress of an investigation. But, of course, you know all about that, don't you? Being a big-city detective. Hmmm?'

167

'I'm sorry if I . . .'

'And of course we're just a bunch of local hicks who don't know nothing at all about police work. Why, we wouldn't even know enough to have a autopsy performed on that little girl, now would we? Or to have tests made of the blood on that chair, now would we? We wouldn't have no crime lab in the next biggest town to Rawson, would we?'

'The way you were handling the investigation . . .' Hawes started.

'. . . was none of your damn business,' Watt concluded. 'Maybe we like to make our own mistakes, Hawes! But naturally, you city cops never make mistakes. That's why there ain't no crime at all where you come from.'

'Look,' Hawes said, 'you were mishandling evidence. I don't give a damn what you . . .'

'As it turns out, it don't matter because there wasn't no fingerprints on that pole, anyway. And we had to get our men up the mountain, so we had to use the lift. There was a hell of a lot of confusion there today, mister. But I don't suppose big-city cops ever get confused, hmmmm?' Watt looked at him sourly. 'Take the cuffs off him, Fred,' he said.

Fred looked surprised, but he unlocked the handcuffs. 'He hit me right in the eye,' he said to Watt.

'Well, you still got the other eye,' Watt said drily. 'Go to bed, Hawes. We had enough of you for one night.'

'What did the autopsy report say?' Hawes asked.

Watt looked at him in something close to astonishment. 'You still sticking your nose in this?'

'I'd still like to help, yes.'

'Maybe we don't need your help.'

'Maybe you can use it. No one here knows . . .'

'There we go with the damn big-city attitu—'

'I was going to say,' Hawes said, overriding Watt's voice, 'that no one in the area knows I'm a cop. That could be helpful to you.'

Watt was silent. 'Maybe,' he said at last.

'*May* I hear the autopsy report?'

Watt was silent again. Then he nodded. He picked up a

sheet of paper from his desk and said, 'Death caused by fatal stab wound of the heart, penetration of the auricles and pulmonary artery. That's where all the blood came from, Hawes. Wounds of the ventricles don't usually bleed that much. Coroner figures the girl died in maybe two or three minutes, there was that much loss of blood.'

'Anything else?'

'Broke her ankle when she fell out of that chair. Oblique fracture of the lateral malleolus. Examiner also found traces of human skin under the girl's fingernails. Seems like she clawed out at whoever stabbed her, and took a goodly part of him away with her.'

'What did the skin tell you?'

'Not a hell of a lot. Our killer is white and adult.'

'That's all?'

'That's all. At least, that's all from the skin, except the possibility of using it later for comparison tests – if we ever get anybody to compare it with. We found traces of blood on her fingers and nails, too, not her own.'

'How do you know?'

'Blood on the chair, the girl's blood, was in the AB grouping. Blood we found on her hands was in the O grouping, most likely the killer's.'

'Then she scratched him enough to cause bleeding.'

'She took a big chunk of skin from him, Hawes.'

'From the face?'

'Now how in hell would I know?'

'I thought maybe . . .'

'Couldn't tell from the skin sample whether it came from the neck or the face or wherever. She coulda scratched him anyplace.'

'Anything else?'

'We found a trail of the girl's blood in the snow under the lift. Plenty of it, believe me, she bled like a stuck pig. The trail started about four minutes from the top. Took her two or three minutes to die. So, assuming the killer jumped from the chair right soon's he stabbed her, then the girl . . .'

'. . . was still alive when he jumped.'

'That's right.'

'Find any tracks in the snow?'

'Nothing. Too many drifts. We don't know whether he jumped with his skis on or not. Have to have been a pretty good skier to attempt that, we figure.'

'Well, anyway, he's got a scratch,' Hawes said. 'That's *something* to look for.'

'You gonna start looking tonight?' Watt asked sarcastically.

11

Blanche Colby was waiting for him when he got back to the room. She was sitting up in his bed propped against the pillows, wearing a shapeless flannel nightgown which covered her from her throat to her ankles. She was holding an apple in her hand, and she bit into it angrily as he entered the room, and then went back to reading the open book in her lap.

'Hi,' he said.

She did not answer him, nor did she even look up at him. She continued destroying the apple, continued her pretence of reading.

'Good book?'

'*Excellent* book,' she answered.

'Miss me?'

'Drop dead,' Blanche said.

'I'm sorry. I ...'

'Don't be. I enjoyed myself immensely in your absence.'

'I got arrested, you see.'

'You got *what*?'

170

'Arrested. Pinched. Pulled in. Collared. Apprehen—'

'I understood you the first time. Who arrested you?'

'The cops,' Hawes said, and he shrugged.

'Serves you right.' She put down the book. 'Wasn't it you who told me a girl was killed on this mountain today? Murdered? And you run off and leave me when a killer ...'

'I told you where I was going. I told you ...'

'You said you'd be back in an hour!'

'Yes, but I didn't know I was going to be arrested.'

'What happened to your cheek?'

'I got hit with a hammer.'

'Good,' Blanche said, and she nodded emphatically.

'Aren't you going to kiss my wound?' Hawes asked.

'*You* can kiss my ...'

'Ah-ah,' he cautioned.

'I sat by that damn fireplace until eleven o'clock. Then I came up here and ... what time is it, anyway?'

'After midnight.'

Blanche nodded again. 'I would have packed up and gone home, believe me, if the roads were open.'

'Yes, but they're closed.'

'Yes, damn it!'

'Aren't you glad I'm back?'

Blanche shrugged. 'I couldn't care less. I was just about to go to sleep.'

'In here?'

'In the other room, naturally.'

'Honey, honey ...'

'Yes, honey-honey?' she mimicked. '*What*, honey-honey baby?'

Hawes grinned. 'That's a very lovely nightgown. My grandmother used to wear a nightgown like that.'

'I thought you'd like it,' Blanche said sourly. 'I put it on especially for you.'

'I always liked the touch of flannel,' he said.

'Get your big hands ...' she started, and moved away from him swiftly. Folding her arms across the front of her gown, she sat in the centre of the bed and stared at the opposite wall.

Hawes studied her for a moment, took off his sweaters, and then began unbuttoning his shirt.

'If you're going to undress,' Blanche said evenly, 'you could at least have the modesty to go into the ...'

'Shhh!' Hawes said sharply. His hands had stopped on the buttons of his shirt. He cocked his head to one side now and listened. Blanche, watching him, frowned.

'What ... ?'

'Shhh!' he said again, and again he listened attentively. The room was silent. Into the silence came the sound.

'Do you hear it?' he asked.

'Do I hear what?'

'Listen.'

They listened together. The sound was unmistakable, faint and faraway, but unmistakable.

'It's the same buzzing I heard last night,' Hawes said. 'I'll be right back.'

'Where are you going?'

'Downstairs. To the ski shop,' he answered, and swiftly left the room. As he went down the corridor towards the steps, a door at the opposite end of the hall opened. A young girl wearing a quilted robe over her pyjamas, her hair done in curlers, came into the hallway carrying a towel and a tooth brush. She smiled at Hawes and then walked past him. He heard the bathroom door locking behind her as he went down the steps.

The lights were on in the ski shop. The buzzing sound came from somewhere in the shop, intermittent, hanging on the silent night air, ceasing abruptly, beginning again. He walked silently over the snow, stopping just outside the door to the shop. He put his ear to the wood and listened, but the only sound he heard was the buzzing. He debated kicking in the door. Instead, he knocked gently.

'Yes?' a voice from inside called.

'Could you open up, please?' Hawes said.

He waited. He could hear the heavy sound of ski boots approaching the locked door. The door opened a crack. A sun-tanned face appeared in the opening. He recognized the face at once – Helmut Kurtz, the ski instructor who had helped him the night before, the man he'd seen today on the mountain just before he'd got on the chair lift.

'Oh, hello there,' Hawes said.

'Yes? What is it?' Kurtz asked.

'Mind if I come in?'

'I'm sorry, no one is allowed in the shop. The shop is closed.'

'Yes, but *you're* in it, aren't you?'

'I'm an instructor,' Kurtz said. 'We are permitted ...'

'I just saw a light,' Hawes said, 'and I felt like talking to someone.'

'Well ...'

'What are you doing, anyway?' Hawes asked casually, and casually he wedged one shoulder against the door and gently eased it open, casually pushing it into the room, casually squeezing his way into the opening, casually shouldering his way past Kurtz and then squinting past the naked hanging light bulb to the work bench at the far end of the room, trying to locate the source of the buzzing sound which filled the shop.

'You are really not allowed ...' Kurtz started, but Hawes was already halfway across the room, moving towards the other small area of light where a green-shaded bulb hung over the work bench. The buzzing sound was louder, the sound of an old machine, the sound of ...

He located it almost at once. A grinding wheel was set up on one end of the bench. The wheel was still spinning. He looked at it, nodded and then flicked the switch to turn it off. Turning to Kurtz, he smiled and said, 'Were you sharpening something?'

'Yes, those skates,' Kurtz said. He pointed to a pair of white figure skates on the bench.

'Yours?' Hawes asked.

Kurtz smiled. 'No. Those are women's skates.'

'Whose?'

'Well, I don't think that is any of your business, do you?' Kurtz asked politely.

'I suppose not,' Hawes answered gently, still smiling. 'Were you in here sharpening something last night, too, Mr Kurtz?'

'I beg your pardon?'

'I said, were you ...'

'No, I was not.' Kurtz walked up to the bench and studied Hawes slowly and deliberately. 'Who *are* you?' he asked.

'My name's Cotton Hawes.'

'How do you do? Mr Hawes, I'm sorry to have to be so abrupt, but you are really not allowed ...'

'Yes, I know. Only instructors are allowed in here, isn't that right, Mr Kurtz?'

'After closing, yes. We sometimes come in to make minor repairs on our skis or ...'

'Or sharpen up some things, huh, Mr Kurtz?'

'Yes. Like the skates.'

'Yes,' Hawes repeated. 'Like the skates. But you weren't in here last night, were you, Mr Kurtz?'

'No, I was not.'

'Because, you see, I heard what could have been the sound of a file or a rasp or something, and then the sound of this grinding wheel. So you're sure you weren't in here sharpening something? Like skates? Or ...' Hawes shrugged. 'A ski pole?'

'A ski pole? Why would anyone ... ?' Kurtz fell suddenly silent. He studied Hawes again. 'What are you?' he asked. 'A policeman?'

'Why? Don't you like policemen?'

'I had nothing to do with Helga's death,' Kurtz said immediately.

'No one said you did.'

'You implied it.'

'I implied nothing, Mr Kurtz.'

'You asked if I were sharpening a ski pole last night. The implication is ...'

'But you weren't.'

'No, I was *not*!' Kurtz said angrily.

'What *were* you sharpening last night?'

'Nothing. I was nowhere near this shop last night.'

'Ahh, but you were, Mr Kurtz. I met you outside, remember? You were coming down the steps. Very fast. Don't you remember?'

'That was earlier in the evening.'

'But I didn't say anything about time, Mr Kurtz. I didn't ask you *when* you were in this shop.'

'I was *not* in this shop! Not at any time!'

'But you just said, "That was earlier in the evening." Earlier than what, Mr Kurtz?'

Kurtz was silent for a moment. Then he said, 'Earlier than ... than whoever was here.'

'You saw someone here?'

'I ... I saw a light burning.'

'When? What time?'

'I don't remember. I went to the bar after I met you ... and I had a few drinks, and then I went for a walk. That was when I saw the light.'

'Where do you room, Mr Kurtz?'

'In the main building.'

'Did you see Helga at any time last night?'

'No.'

'Not at any time?'

'No.'

'Then what were you doing upstairs?'

'I came to get Maria's skates. Those.' He pointed to the figure skates on the bench.

'Maria who?'

'Maria Fiers.'

'Is she a small girl with dark hair?'

'Yes. Do you know her?'

'I think I just saw her in the hallway,' Hawes said. 'So you came to get her skates, and then you went for a drink, and then you went for a walk. What time was that?'

'It must have been after midnight.'

'And a light was burning in the ski shop?'

'Yes.'

'But you didn't see who was in here?'

'No, I did not.'

'How well did you know Helga?'

'Very well. We taught together.'

'How well is very well?'

'We were good friends.'

'How good, Mr Kurtz?'

'I *told* you!'

'Were you sleeping with her?'

'How dare you ...'

'Okay, okay.' Hawes pointed to the skates. 'These are Maria's, you said?'

'Yes. She's an instructor here, too. But she skates well, almost as well as she skis.'

'Are you good friends with her, too, Mr Kurtz?'

'I am good friends with *everyone*!' Kurtz said angrily. 'I am normally a friendly person.' He paused. '*Are* you a policeman?'

'Yes. I am.'

'I don't like policemen,' Kurtz said, his voice low. 'I didn't like them in Vienna, where they wore swastikas on their arms, and I don't like them here, either. I had nothing to do with Helga's death.'

'Do you have a key to this shop, Mr Kurtz?'

'Yes. We *all* do. We make our own minor repairs. During the day, there are too many people here. At night, we can ...'

'What do you mean by *all*? The instructors?'

'Yes.'

'I see. Then any of the instructors could have ...'

The scream was a sentient thing which invaded the room suddenly and startlingly. It came from somewhere upstairs, ripping down through the ancient floor boards and the ancient ceiling timbers. It struck the room with its blunt force, and both men looked up towards the ceiling, speechless, waiting. The scream came again. Hawes got to his feet and ran for the door. '*Blanche*,' he whispered, and slammed the door behind him.

She was standing in the corridor outside the hall bathroom, not really standing, but leaning limply against the wall, her supporting dancer's legs robbed of stance, robbed of control.

She wore the long flannel nightgown with a robe over it, and she leaned against the wall with her eyes shut tight, her blonde hair disarrayed, the scream unvoiced now, but frozen in the set of her face and the trembling openness of her mouth. Hawes came stamping up the steps and turned abruptly right, and stopped stock still when he saw her, an interruption of movement for only a fraction of a second, the turn, the stop, and then a forward motion again which carried him to her in four headlong strides.

'What is it?' he said.

She could not answer. She clung to the wall with the flat palms of her hands, her eyes still squeezed shut tightly, the scream frozen in her throat and blocking articulation. She shook her head.

'Blanche, what is it?'

She shook her head again, and then pulled one hand from the wall, as if afraid that by doing so she would lose her grip and tumble to the floor. The hand rose limply. It did not point, it only indicated, and that in the vaguest manner, as if it too were dazed.

'The bathroom?' he asked.

She nodded. He turned from her. The bathroom door was partly open. He opened it the rest of the way, rushing into the room, and then stopping instantly, as if he had run into a stone wall.

Maria Fiers was inside her clothing and outside of it. The killer had caught her either dressing or undressing, had caught her in what she supposed was privacy, so that one leg was in the trousers of her pyjamas and the other lay twisted beneath her body, naked. Her pyjama top had ridden up over one delicately curved breast, perhaps as she fell, perhaps as she struggled. Even her hair seemed in a state of uncertain transition, some of it held firmly in place by curlers, the rest hanging in haphazard abandon, the loose curlers scattered on the bathroom floor. The hook latch on the inside of the door had been ripped from the jamb when the door was forced. The water in the sink was still running. The girl lay still and dead in her invaded privacy, partially clothed, partially disrobed,

surprise and terror wedded in the death mask of her face. A
towel was twisted about her throat. It had been twisted there
with tremendous force, biting into the skin with such power
that it remained twisted there now, the flesh torn and over-
lapping it in places, the coarse cloth almost embedded into
her neck and throat. Her tongue protruded from her mouth.
She was bleeding from her nose where her face had struck the
bathroom tile in falling.

He backed out of the room.

He found a pay telephone in the main building, and from
there he called Theodore Watt.

12

Blanche sat on the edge of the bed in room 105, shivering
inside her gown, her robe, and a blanket which had been
thrown over her shoulders. Theodore Watt leaned disjointedly
against the dresser, puffed on his cigar, and said, 'Now you
want to tell me exactly what happened, Miss Colby?'

Blanche sat shivering and hunched, her face pale. She
searched for her voice, seemed unable to find it, shook her
head, nodded, cleared her throat, and seemed surprised that
she could speak. 'I ... I was alone. Cotton had gone down to
see what ... what the noise was.'

'What noise, Hawes?' Watt asked.

'A grinding wheel,' he answered. 'Downstairs in the ski
shop. I heard it last night, too.'

'Did you find who was running the wheel?'

'Tonight, it was a guy named Helmut Kurtz. He's an instructor here, too. Claims he was nowhere near the shop last
night. But he did see a light burning after midnight.'

'Where's he now?'

'I don't know. Sheriff, he was with me when the girl was killed. He couldn't possibly have ...'

Watt ignored him and walked to the door. He opened it, and leaned into the corridor. 'Fred,' he said, 'find me Helmut Kurtz, an instructor here.'

'I got that other guy from down the hall,' Fred answered.

'I'll be right with him. Tell him to wait.'

'What other guy?' Hawes asked.

'Instructor in 102. Larry Davidson.' Watt shook his head. 'Place is crawling with goddamn instructors, excuse me, miss. Wonder there's any room for guests.' He shook his head again. 'You said you were alone, Miss Colby.'

'Yes. And I ... I thought I heard something down the hall ... like ... I didn't know what. A loud sudden noise.'

'Probably the bathroom door being kicked in,' Watt said. 'Go on.'

'And then I ... I heard a girl's voice saying, "Get out of here! Do you hear me? Get out of here!" And ... and it was quiet, and I heard someone running down the hall and down the steps, so I ... I thought I ought to ... to look.'

'Yes, go on.'

'I went down the ... the hallway and looked down the steps, but I didn't see anyone. And then, when I ... when I was starting back for the room, I ... I heard the water running in the bathroom. The ... the door was open, so I ... Oh Jesus, do I *have* to?'

'You found the girl, is that right?'

'Yes,' Blanche said, her voice very low.

'And then you screamed.'

'Yes.'

'And then Hawes came upstairs, is that right?'

'Yes,' Hawes said. 'And I called you from the main building.'

'Um-huh,' Watt said. He went to the door and opened it. 'Want to come in here, Mr Davidson?' he asked.

Larry Davidson came into the room hesitantly. He was a tall man, and he stooped as he came through the doorway, giving an impression of even greater height, as if he had to stoop to avoid the top of the door frame. He was wearing dark trousers and a plaid woollen sports shirt. His hair was clipped close to his scalp. His blue eyes were alert, if not wary.

'Guess you know what this is all about, huh, Mr Davidson?' Watt asked.

'Yes, I think so,' Davidson answered.

'You don't mind answering a few questions, do you?'

'No. I'll ... I'll answer anything you ...'

'Fine. Were you in your room all night, Mr Davidson?'

'Not all night, no. I was up at the main building part of the time.'

'Doing what?'

'Well, I ...'

'Yes, Mr Davidson, what were you doing?'

'I ... I was fencing. Look, I didn't have anything to do with this.'

'You were *what*, Mr Davidson?'

'Fencing. We've got some foils and masks up there, and I ... I was just fooling around. Look, I *know* Helga was stabbed, but ...'

'What time did you get back here, Mr Davidson?'

'About ... about ten-thirty, eleven.'

'And you've been in your room since then?'

'Yes.'

'What did you do when you got back here?'

'I wrote a letter to my wife, and then I went to sleep.'

'What time did you go to sleep?'

'About midnight.'

'Did you hear any loud noise in the hall?'

'No.'

'Did you hear any voices?'

'No.'

'Did you hear Miss Colby when she screamed?'

'No.'

'Why not?'

'I guess I was asleep.'

'You sleep in your clothes, Mr Davidson?'

'What? Oh. Oh, no. Your fellow ... your deputy said I could put on some clothes.'

'What *were* you sleeping in?'

'My pyjamas. Listen, I barely knew those girls. I only joined the school here two weeks ago. I mean, I knew them to talk to, but that's all. And the fencing is just a coincidence. I mean, we always fool around with the foils. I mean, ever since I came here, somebody's been up there fooling around with ...'

'How many times did you scream, Miss Colby?' Watt asked.

'I don't remember,' Blanche said.

'She screamed twice,' Hawes said.

'Where were you when you heard the screams, Hawes?'

'Downstairs. In the ski shop.'

'But you were in your room, right down the hall, Mr Davidson, and you didn't hear anything, hmmm? Maybe you were too busy ...'

And suddenly Davidson began crying. His face twisted into a grimace, and the tears began flowing, and he said, 'I didn't have anything to do with this, I swear. Please, I didn't have anything to do with it. Please, I'm married, my wife's in the city expecting a baby, I *need* this job, I didn't even *look* at those girls, I swear to God, what do you want me to do? Please, please.'

The room was silent except for his sobbing.

'I swear to God,' he said softly. 'I swear to God. I'm a heavy sleeper. I'm very tired at night. I swear. Please. I didn't do it. I only knew them to say hello. I didn't hear anything. Please. Believe me. Please. I *have* to keep this job. It's the only thing I know, skiing. I can't get involved in this. Please.'

He lowered his head, trying to hide the tears that streamed down his face, his shoulders heaving, the deep sobs starting deep inside him and reverberating through his entire body.

'Please,' he said.

For the first time since the whole thing had started, Watt turned to Hawes and asked his advice.

'What do you think?' he said.

'I'm a heavy sleeper, too,' Hawes said. 'You could blow up the building, and I wouldn't hear it.'

13

On Sunday morning, the church bells rang out over the valley.

They started in the town of Rawson, and they rang sharp and clear on the mountain air, drifting over the snow and down the valley. He went to the window and pulled up the shade, and listened to the sound of the bells, and remembered his own youth and the Reverend Jeremiah Hawes who had been his father, and the sound of Sunday church bells, and the rolling, sonorous voice of his father delivering the sermon. There had always been logic in his father's sermons. Hawes had not come away from his childhood background with any abiding religious fervour – but he had come away with a great respect for logic. 'To be believed,' his father had told him, 'it must be reasonable. And to be reasonable, it must be logical. You could do worse than remembering that, Cotton.'

There did not seem to be much logic in the killing of Helga Nilson and Maria Fiers, unless there was logic in wanton brutality. He tried to piece together the facts as he looked out over the peaceful valley and listened to the steady tolling of the bells. Behind him, Blanche was curled in sleep, gently breathing, her arms wrapped around the pillow. He did not want to wake her yet, not after what she'd been through last night. So far as he was concerned, the weekend was over; he could not ski with pleasure any more, not this weekend. He wanted nothing more than to get away from Rawson Mountain, no, that wasn't quite true. He wanted to find the killer. That was what he wanted more than anything else. Not because he was being paid for the job, not because he wanted to prove to Theodore Watt that maybe big-city detectives *did* have a little something on the ball – but only because the double murders filled him with a sense of outrage. He could still remember the animal strength of the man who'd attacked him on the mountain, and the thought of that power directed against two helpless young girls angered Hawes beyond all reason.

Why? he asked himself.

Where is the logic?

There was none. No logic in the choice of the victims, and no logic in the choice of the scene. Why would anyone have chosen to kill Helga in broad daylight, on a chair suspended anywhere from six to thirty feet above the ground, using a ski pole as a weapon? A ski pole sharpened to a deadly point, Hawes reminded himself, don't forget that. This thing didn't just happen, this was no spur-of-the-moment impulse, this was planned and premeditated, a pure and simple Murder One. Somebody had been in that ski shop the night before the first murder, using a file and then a grinding wheel, sharpening that damn pole, making certain its end could penetrate a heavy ski parka, *and* a ski sweater, *and* a heart.

Then there must have been logic to the choice of locale, Hawes thought. Whoever killed Helga had at least planned far enough ahead to have prepared a weapon the night before. And admitting the existence of a plan, then logic could be presupposed, and it could further be assumed that killing her on the chair lift was a *part* of the plan – perhaps a very necessary part of it.

Yes, that's logic, he thought – *except that it's illogical.*

Behind him, Blanche stirred. He turned to look at her briefly, remembering the horror on her face last night, contrasting it now with her features relaxed in sleep. She had told the story to Watt three times, had told him again and again how she'd found the dead girl.

Maria Fiers, twenty-one years old, brunette, a native of Montpelier, Vermont. She had begun skiing when she was six years old, had won the women's slalom four times running, had been an instructor since she was seventeen. She skated, too, and had been on her high school swimming team, an all-round athlete, a nice girl with a gentle manner and a pleasant smile – dead.

Why?

She lived in the room next door to Helga's, had known Helga for close to a year. She had been nowhere near the chair lift on the day Helga was killed. In fact, she had been teaching a beginners' class near the T-Bar, a good distance from the chair lift. She could not have seen Helga's murder, nor Helga's murderer.

But someone had killed her nonetheless.

And if there were a plan, and if there were supposed logic to the plan, and if killing Helga on a chair halfway up the mountain was part of that logic, then the death of Maria Fiers was also a part of it.

But how?

The hell with it, Hawes thought. I can't think straight any more. I want to crack this so badly that I can't think straight, and that makes me worse than useless. So the thing to do is to get out of here, wake Blanche and tell her to dress and pack, and then pay my bill and get out, back to the city, back to the 87th where death comes more frequently perhaps, and just as brutally – but not as a surprise. I'll leave this to Theodore Watt, the sheriff who wants to make his own mistakes. I'll leave it to him and his nimble-fingered deputies, and maybe they'll bust it wide open, or maybe they won't, but it's too much for me, I can't think straight any more.

He went to the bed and woke Blanche, and then he walked over to the main building, anxious to pay his bill and get on his way. Someone was at the piano, practising scales. Hawes walked past the piano and the fireplace and around the corner to Wollender's office. He knocked on the door, and waited. There was a slight hesitation on the other side of the door, and then Wollender said, 'Yes, come in,' and Hawes turned the knob.

Everything looked exactly the way it had looked when Hawes checked in on Friday night, an eternity ago. Wollender was sitting behind his desk, a man in his late twenties with dark hair and dark brows pulled low over deep brown eyes. He was wearing a white shirt open at the throat, a bold reindeer-imprinted sweater over it. The plaster cast was still on his right leg, the leg stretched out stiffly in front of him, the foot resting on a low ottoman. Everything looked exactly the same.

'I want to pay my bill,' Hawes said. 'We're checking out.'

He stood just inside the door, some fifteen feet from the desk. Wollender's crutches leaned against the wall near the door. There was a smile on Wollender's face as he said, 'Certainly,' and then opened the bottom drawer of the desk and took out his register and carefully made out a bill. Hawes walked to the desk, added the bill, and then wrote a cheque. As he waved it in the air to dry the ink, he said, 'What *were* you doing in my room yesterday, Mr Wollender?'

'Checking the heat,' Wollender said.

Hawes nodded. 'Here's your cheque. Will you mark this bill "Paid", please?'

'Be happy to,' Wollender said. He stamped the bill and handed it back to Hawes. For a moment, Hawes had the oddest feeling that something was wrong. The knowledge pushed itself into his mind in the form of an absurd caption: WHAT'S WRONG WITH THIS PICTURE? He looked at Wollender, at his hair, and his eyes, and his white shirt, and his reindeer sweater, and his extended leg, and the cast on it, and the ottoman. Something was different. This was not the room, not the picture as it had been on Friday night. WHAT'S WRONG WITH THIS PICTURE? he thought, and he did not know.

He took the bill. 'Thanks,' he said. 'Have you heard any news about the roads?'

'They're open all the way to the Thruway. You shouldn't have any trouble.'

'Thanks,' Hawes said. He hesitated, staring at Wollender. 'My room's right over the ski shop, you know,' he said.

'Yes, I know that.'

'Do you have a key to the shop, Mr Wollender?'

Wollender shook his head. 'No. The shop is privately

owned. It doesn't belong to the hotel. I believe the proprietor allows the ski instructors to . . .'

'But then, you're a locksmith, aren't you?'

'What?'

'Isn't that what you told me when I checked in? You said you were a locksmith out of season, didn't you?'

'Oh. Oh, yes. Yes, I did.' Wollender shifted uneasily in the chair, trying to make his leg comfortable. Hawes looked at the leg again, and then he thought, Damn it, what's wrong?

'Maybe you went to my room to listen, Mr Wollender. Is that possible?'

'Listen to what?'

'To the sounds coming from the ski shop below,' Hawes said.

'Are the sounds that interesting?'

'In the middle of the night, they are. You can hear all sorts of things in the middle of the night. I'm just beginning to remember all the things I heard.'

'Oh? What did you hear?'

'I heard the oil burner clicking, and the toilet flushing, and the Cats going up the mountain, and someone arguing down the hall, and somebody filing and grinding in the ski shop.' He was speaking to Wollender, but not really speaking to him. He was, instead, remembering those midnight voices raised in anger, and remembering that it was only later he had heard the noises in the shop, and gone to the window, and seen the light burning below. And then a curious thing happened. Instead of calling him 'Mr Wollender', he suddenly called him 'Elmer'.

'Elmer,' he said, 'something's just occurred to me.'

Elmer. And with the word, something new came into the room. With the word, he was suddenly transported back to the interrogation room at the 87th, where common thieves and criminals were called by their first names, Charlie, and Harry, and Martin, and Joe, and where this familiarity somehow put them on the defensive, somehow rattled them and made them know their questioners weren't playing games.

'Elmer,' he said, leaning over the desk, 'it's just occurred to me that since Maria couldn't have *seen* anything on the mountain, maybe she was killed because she *heard* something. And maybe what she heard was the same arguing I heard. Only *her* room is right next door to Helga's. And maybe she knew *who* was arguing.' He hesitated. 'That's pretty logical, don't you think, Elmer?'

'I suppose so,' Wollender said pleasantly. 'But if you know who killed Maria, why don't you go to . . .'

'I don't know, Elmer. Do *you* know?'

'I'm sorry. I don't.'

'Yeah, neither do I, Elmer. All I have is a feeling.'

'And what's the feeling?' Wollender asked.

'That you came to my room to listen, Elmer. To find out how much *I* had heard the night before Helga was murdered. And maybe you decided I heard too damn much, and maybe that's why I was attacked on the mountain yesterday.'

'Please, Mr Hawes,' Wollender said, and a faint superior smile touched his mouth, and his hand opened limply to indicate the leg in the cast.

'Sure, sure,' Hawes said. 'How could I have been attacked by a man with his leg in a cast, a man who can't get around without crutches? Sure, Elmer. Don't think that hasn't been bugg—' He stopped dead. 'Your crutches,' he said.

'What?'

'Your crutches! Where the hell are they?'

For just an instant, the colour went out of Wollender's face. Then, quite calmly, he said, 'Right over there. Behind you.'

Hawes turned and looked at the crutches, leaning against the wall near the door.

'Fifteen feet from your desk,' he said. 'I thought you couldn't walk without them.'

'I . . . I used the furniture to . . . to get to the desk. I . . .'

'You're lying, Elmer,' Hawes said, and he reached across the desk and pulled Wollender out of the chair.

'My leg!' Wollender shouted.

'Your leg, my ass! How long have you been walking on it, Elmer? Was that why you killed her on the mountain? So that . . .'

'I didn't kill anybody!'

'... so that you'd have a perfect alibi? A man with his leg in a cast couldn't possibly ride a lift or jump from it, could he? Unless he'd been in and out of that cast for God knows how long!'

'My leg is broken! I can't walk!'

'Can you *kill*, Elmer?'

'I didn't kill her!'

'Did Maria hear you arguing, Elmer?'

'No. No ...'

'Then why'd you go after her?'

'I didn't!' He tried to pull away from Hawes. 'You're crazy. You're hurting my leg! Let go of ...'

'*I'm* crazy? You son of a bitch, *I'm* crazy? You stuck a ski pole in one girl and twisted a towel around ...'

'I didn't, I didn't!'

'We found the basket from your pole!' Hawes shouted.

'What basket? I don't know what ...'

'Your fingerprints are all over it!' he lied.

'You're crazy,' Wollender said. 'How could I get on the lift? I can't walk. I broke the leg in two places. One of the bones came right through the skin. I couldn't get on a lift if I wanted ...'

'The skin,' Hawes said.

'What?'

'The skin!' There was a wild look in his eyes now. He pulled Wollender closer to him and yelled, 'Where'd she scratch you?'

'What?'

He seized the front of Wollender's shirt with both hands, and then ripped it open. 'Where's the cut, Elmer? On your chest? On your neck?'

Wollender struggled to get away from him, but Hawes had his head captured in both huge hands now. He twisted Wollender's face viciously, forced his head forward, pulled back the shirt collar.

'Let go of me!' Wollender screamed.

'What's this, Elmer?' His fingers grasped the adhesive

188

bandage on the back of Wollender's neck. Angrily, he tore it loose. A healing cut, two inches long and smeared with iodine, ran diagonally from a spot just below Wollender's hairline.

'I did that myself,' Wollender said. 'I bumped into ...'

'Helga did it,' Hawes said. 'When you stabbed her! The sheriff's got the skin, Elmer. It was under her fingernails.'

'No,' Wollender said. He shook his head.

The room was suddenly very still. Both men were exhausted. Hawes kept clinging to the front of Wollender's shirt, breathing hard, waiting. Wollender kept shaking his head.

'You want to tell me?'

Wollender shook his head.

'How long have you been walking?'

Wollender shook his head again.

'Why'd you keep your leg in the cast?'

Again, Wollender shook his head.

'*You killed two young girls!*' Hawes bellowed. He was surprised to find himself trembling. His hand tightened on the shirt front, the knuckles showing white through his skin. Perhaps Wollender felt the sudden tension, perhaps Wollender knew that in the next instant Hawes would throttle him.

'All right,' he said. His voice was very low. 'All right.'

'Why'd you keep wearing the cast?'

'So ... so ... so she wouldn't know. So she would think I ... I was ... was unable to walk. And that way, I could ... could watch her. Without her knowing.'

'Watch who?'

'Helga. She ... She was my girl, you see. I ... I loved her, you see.'

'Yeah, you loved her enough to kill her,' Hawes said.

'That's *not* why I ...' He shook his head. 'It was because of Kurtz. She kept denying it, but I knew about them. And I warned her. You have to believe that I warned her. And I ... I kept the cast on my leg to ... to fool her.'

'When did it come off?' Hawes asked.

'Last week. The ... the doctor took it off right in this room. He did a bivalve, with an electric saw, cut it right down the side. And . . . and when he was gone, I . . . I figured I could put the two halves together again, and . . . and . . . hold it in place with . . . with tape. That way, I could watch her. Without her knowing I could get around.'

'And what did you see?'

'You *know* what I saw!'

'Tell me.'

'Friday night, she . . . I . . . I saw Kurtz leaving the annexe. I knew he'd been with her.'

'He was there to pick up Maria's skates,' Hawes said. 'To sharpen them.'

'No!' Wollender shouted, and for a moment there was force in his voice, a vocal explosion, fury and power, and Hawes remembered again the brute strength of Wollender's attack on the mountain. Wollender's voice died again. 'No,' he said softly, 'you're mistaken. He was with Helga. I know. Do you think I'd have killed her if . . .' His voice caught. His eyes suddenly misted. He turned his head, not looking at Hawes, staring across the room, the tears solidifying his eyes. 'When I went up to her room, I warned her,' he said, his voice low. 'I told her I had seen him, seen him with my own eyes, and she . . . she said I was imagining things. And she laughed.' His face went suddenly tight. 'She laughed, you see. She . . . she shouldn't have laughed.' His eyes filled with tears, had a curiously opaque look. 'She shouldn't have laughed,' he said. 'It wasn't funny. I loved her. It wasn't funny.'

'No,' Hawes said wearily. 'It wasn't funny at all.'

14

The storm was over.

The storm which had started suddenly and filled the air with fury was gone. The wind had died after scattering the clouds from the sky. They drove in the warm comfort of the convertible, the sky a clear blue ahead of them, the snow banked on either side of the road.

The storm was over.

There were only the remains of its fury now, the hard-packed snow beneath the automobile, and the snow lining the roads, and the snow hanging in the branches of the trees. But now it was over and done, and now there was only the damage to count, and the repairs to be made.

He sat silently behind the wheel of the car, a big redheaded man who drove effortlessly. His anger was gone, too, like the anger of the storm. There was only a vast sadness inside him.

'Cotton?' Blanche said.

'Mmmm?' He did not take his eyes from the road. He watched the winding white ribbon and listened to the crunch of snow beneath his heavy-duty tyres, and over that the sound of her voice.

'Cotton,' she said, 'I'm very glad to be with you.'

'I am, too.'

'In spite of everything,' she said, 'I'm very, very glad.'

He did a curious thing then. He suddenly took his right hand from the wheel and put it on her thigh, and squeezed her gently. He thought he did it because Blanche was a very attractive girl with whom he had just shared a moment of communication.

But perhaps he touched her because death had suddenly shouldered its way into that automobile, and he had remembered again the two young girls who had been Wollender's victims.

Perhaps he touched her thigh, soft and warm, only as a reaffirmation of life.

Bestselling Fiction and Non-Fiction

☐ **The Amityville Horror**	Jay Anson	80p
☐ **Shadow of the Wolf**	James Barwick	95p
☐ **The Island**	Peter Benchley	£1.25p
☐ **Castle Raven**	Laura Black	£1.25p
☐ **Smart-Aleck Kill**	Raymond Chandler	95p
☐ **Sphinx**	Robin Cook	£1.25p
☐ **The Entity**	Frank De Felitta	£1.25p
☐ **Trial Run**	Dick Francis	95p
☐ **The Rich are Different**	Susan Howatch	£1.95p
☐ **Moviola**	Garson Kanin	£1.50p
☐ **Tinker Tailor Soldier Spy**	John le Carré	£1.50p
☐ **The Empty Copper Sea**	John D. MacDonald	90p
☐ **Where There's Smoke**	Ed McBain	80p
☐ **The Master Mariner** Book 1: Running Proud	Nicholas Monsarrat	£1.50p
☐ **Bad Blood**	Richard Neville and Julie Clarke	£1.50p
☐ **Victoria in the Wings**	Jean Plaidy	£1.25p
☐ **Fools Die**	Mario Puzo	£1.50p
☐ **Sunflower**	Marilyn Sharp	95p
☐ **The Throwback**	Tom Sharpe	95p
☐ **Wild Justice**	Wilbur Smith	£1.50p
☐ **That Old Gang of Mine**	Leslie Thomas	£1.25p
☐ **Caldo Largo**	Earl Thompson	£1.50p
☐ **Harvest of the Sun**	E. V. Thompson	£1.25p
☐ **Future Shock**	Alvin Toffler	£1.95p

All these books are available at your local bookshop or newsagent, or can be ordered direct from the publisher. Indicate the number of copies required and fill in the form below

Name_____
(block letters please)
Address_____

Send to Pan Books (CS Department), Cavaye Place, London SW10 9PG
Please enclose remittance to the value of the cover price plus:

25p for the first book plus 10p per copy for each additional book ordered to a maximum charge of £1.05 to cover postage and packing Applicable only in the UK

While every effort is made to keep prices low, it is sometimes necessary to increase prices at short notice. Pan Books reserve the right to show on covers and charge new retail prices which may differ from those advertised in the text or elsewhere